He Was Playing Her.

Fine. She could play, too. She could make him sorry he'd ever pulled her into his game. She grabbed a handful of his jacket, raised herself on tiptoe, wrapped one arm around his neck and pressed her mouth to his.

She was determined that this last a whole lot longer than that brief kiss they'd shared before. She wanted to teach him a lesson.

After a second of hesitation, Todd put his arms around her and kissed her back. He moved purposefully, like a man on a mission. There was so much heat and need and pleasure, she let him have his way and was rewarded when he kissed his way down her neck....

Dear Reader,

Poor Todd Aston III. His very favorite aunt-by-marriage offered each of her granddaughters a million dollars if one of them would marry him. Talk about humiliating. He doesn't need help getting women. He's successful, wealthy, good-looking. He could be married ten times over if that's what he wanted. In his world, women are only out for what they can get, and what they usually want is his money.

There's one unattached granddaughter left, but if he can avoid her, the problem is solved. Except he and Marina Nelson have agreed to plan a wedding together. There's nothing like a beautiful woman in a wedding dress to get a guy's attention.

Marina has no interest in Todd. She agreed to the million-dollar deal as a joke—honestly, she would never marry for money. But when she starts to fall for Todd—something she never saw coming—disaster lurks. Will a man who's been chased by women all his life believe she's in it only for his heart?

Susan Mallery

SUSAN MALLERY

THE ULTIMATE MILLIONAIRE

Published by Silhouette Books

America's Publisher of Contemporary Romance

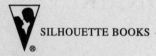 SILHOUETTE BOOKS

ISBN-13: 978-0-373-76772-4
ISBN-10:   0-373-76772-2

THE ULTIMATE MILLIONAIRE

Copyright © 2007 by Susan Macias Redmond

This edition published by arrangement with Harlequin Books S.A.

® and TM are trademarks of Harlequin Books S.A., used under license. Trademarks indicated with ® are registered in the United States Patent and Trademark Office, the Canadian Trade Marks Office and in other countries.

Visit Silhouette Books at www.eHarlequin.com

Printed in U.S.A.

Recent Books by Susan Mallery

Silhouette Desire

**The Substitute Millionaire* #1760
**The Unexpected Millionaire* #1767
**The Ultimate Millionaire* #1772

Silhouette Special Edition

The Sheik & the Princess in Waiting #1606
The Sheik & the Princess Bride #1647
The Sheik & the Bride Who Said No #1666
The Sheik and the Virgin Secretary #1723
Prodigal Son #1729
‡*Having Her Boss's Baby* #1759
‡*The Ladies' Man* #1778

Harlequin Next

There's Always Plan B #1

**The Million Dollar Catch
*Desert Rogues
‡Positively Pregnant

SUSAN MALLERY

is the bestselling and award-winning author of over fifty
books for Harlequin Books and Silhouette Books. She
makes her home in the Los Angeles area with her handsome prince of a husband and her two adorable-but-not-
bright cats.

One

"Would you do it if I beg?"

Marina Nelson was careful to keep from smiling at Julie's dramatic plea. Of course she was going to agree to help her sister, but not right away. After twenty-four years of being the baby of the family, it was nice to finally have a little power.

"You know I'm busy," she said slowly. "It's the start of a new quarter and I have a full class schedule."

Julie sighed. "Yes, and your work is very important. But so is this. I wouldn't ask if it wasn't. I really need someone to take charge while I'm on this business trip. We have similar taste and you're organized and I thought…" Julie tucked her blond hair behind her ears and looked sad. "Am I asking too much? I am. I know it's crazy. I'm the one getting married, not you. So I should do the planning. But this trip to China is a once-in-a-lifetime opportunity. Six weeks of Ryan and I working together before we settle in to being married *and* parents."

Marina glanced down at her sister's stomach. Julie was only about three months along and not showing at all. One of the advantages of being tall, she thought humorously—it takes longer to see the bump.

"I can see how a trip to China would be far more thrilling than the messy details of choosing a menu and picking out flowers," she said, still not allowing herself to smile. "Not to mention deciding on a dress. What if you hate what I pick?"

They were close enough in size for the actual gown itself not to be a problem. Any minor tailoring could be done right before the wedding, after Julie got back.

"I won't," Julie promised earnestly. "I swear, I'll love it. Besides, you'll send me pictures, right? We talked about that. You'll upload them into e-mail and I'll write back with my opinion." Her blue eyes widened. "Marina, please say yes."

Marina sighed heavily. "No. I can't. But thanks for asking."

Julie's mouth dropped open, then she reached behind her for one of the small, floral sofa cushions and swatted Marina with it.

"You're horrible! How could you let me go on and on like that? I was practically begging."

Marina laughed, then grabbed the cushion. "There's

no 'practically,' Julie. You begged. You whined. I have to tell you, I was a little embarrassed for you."

Julie sighed. "So you'll do it?"

"Of course. You're my sister. Just give me a list and I'll take care of everything."

"You have no idea how you're helping. Between getting married and our trip and closing on the new house, my life is a nightmare."

They sat in Ryan's study—an uncomfortably modern condo in West Los Angeles. It had a great view and electronic everything, but it lacked color and soul, except for a few throw pillows Julie had contributed. Rather than try to make it homey, Julie and Ryan had decided to buy another house that they both liked. Marina knew that Willow, their middle sister, was going to oversee the minor renovating Julie and Ryan's new place needed, which left the wedding to Marina.

"I think of this project as practice," Marina said with a grin. "I can figure out what I want and don't want should I ever take the plunge."

"Oh, please. You'll get married," Julie said confidently. "The right guy's out there somewhere. You'll find him."

Marina wasn't currently looking, but it would be great when it happened. Assuming she could trust herself to fall in love without losing her soul in the process.

"Until then, just call me the wedding planner," Marina said. "Now, where's that list of yours?"

Julie reached into her purse, then straightened without removing anything. "There's just one other thing."

"Which is…"

Julie drew in a breath. "Okay, so this is Ryan's wedding, too, and he's a little nervous that it's going to be too girly. He wants a vote in what's happening."

Marina didn't get the problem. "Fine. You two can argue all you want, then e-mail me the compromise. I don't care."

"Um, yes, well, that's not exactly the plan. Ryan wants a representative to be with you for all the important decisions. The food, the cake, the band, the decorations, the flowers."

"A representative? Like his mother?"

Marina had never met the woman. No doubt she was perfectly lovely, but another opinion could seriously slow the process.

Julie tried to smile and failed miserably. "Actually, no. More like Todd."

"Todd? As in Todd Aston the Third, all around rich guy and jerk?" Marina couldn't believe it. "Anyone but him," she muttered.

"He's Ryan's cousin and they're as close as brothers. You know that. Todd is the best man and he offered to help. Do you hate me now?"

"No, but I should." Marina sighed. "Todd? Yuck."

Nearly six months ago, the three sisters had been introduced to their maternal grandmother for the first time in their lives. Grandma Ruth had been estranged from her only daughter, the girls' mother, ever since Naomi had run off and gotten married.

Now Ruth was back and she wanted a relationship with her daughter and granddaughters. In addition, she had a burning need to connect her family with her second husband's family through marriage.

In a moment of dinner conversation that Marina was confident would go down in family history, she'd offered each of her granddaughters a million dollars if one of them would please marry Todd Aston the Third, her nephew—or maybe great-nephew, no one was sure—through marriage.

Julie had fallen in love with Ryan and Willow had found Kane Dennison, which left only Marina for toady Todd. Talk about bad luck.

For reasons she was still trying to figure out—maybe it had been a momentary brain injury—Marina had agreed to one date with the obnoxious Todd.

It's not that the guy wasn't good-looking—at least, that's what Marina had heard. She'd never actually seen the man. He was also wealthy and successful in his own right, rather than just inheriting from Mommy and Daddy. Ryan liked him and Marina thought Ryan was okay—especially after he'd shown the good taste to fall for her sister. But Todd?

His idea of a significant relationship was to date the same woman twice in the same week. He went out with models. How could she ever have a serious conversation with a man who dated women who were paid to starve for a living? It violated the female code.

Plus, initially he'd tried to break up Julie and Ryan. Marina thought that was pretty low.

"I'm not asking you to have his baby," Julie said. "Just work with him on the wedding. Besides, it won't be too bad. He's a guy. He'll get bored at the first meeting with the florist and disappear. You'll have to deal with him once. Twice at the most."

"I don't want to deal with him at all," Marina said mournfully. "He's everything I don't like in a man." Talk about emotionally useless. Or so she imagined.

A sound came from the doorway. It sounded like someone clearing his throat. When Marina looked up she found a pretty good-looking guy leaning against the door frame.

He looked more amused than annoyed, but based on Julie's gasp and sudden blush, Marina was willing to go out on a limb and figure this was the infamous Todd Aston.

"Ladies," he said with a nod. "Ryan let me in and said you were meeting in here. I've shown up for wedding duty. I'm also accepting a humanitarian award at the end of the month. Perhaps the two of you would like a shot at writing my bio for the event. It would certainly be entertaining."

"Oh, man," Julie muttered. "I'm sorry. That all came out more harshly than I meant it to."

Marina studied him. He was the walking, breathing definition of tall, dark and hunky. Great face with soulful eyes and the kind of mouth that made a woman dream about being taken against her will. Broad shoulders, a muscled chest and jeans skimming over narrow hips and yummy thighs. All in all, a great package. Too bad Todd's personality was stuck inside it.

He smiled at her. "You must be Marina."

"I am. Nice to meet you, Todd."

"Nice?" He raised one eyebrow. "That's not what I heard. You've already decided I'm an ass. Or is it an idiot?"

She shifted on the sofa, feeling just a tiny bit uncomfortable. "You go out with models. Their airbrushed perfection in magazines make regular women feel bad about themselves."

"Because of that, models shouldn't be allowed to date?"

Logic? He wanted to use logic in a discussion about the objectification of thin, young women in modern society?

"Of course they should be allowed to date," she said smoothly. "I'm simply not interested in someone who's interested in them."

"Right," he said folding his arms over his chest. "Because you assume that if they're beautiful they must be dumb. Therefore I like dumb women."

"I didn't say that, but thanks for clarifying."

His mouth twitched as if he were holding in a smile. "I don't date dumb women."

"You should probably make up your mind about that," she told him.

"I'll get right on it."

"If you two are finished…" Julie pointed to the chair opposite the sofa. "Okay, then. So, we should get started with all this. The wedding."

Todd strolled across the room and took the seat offered, then pulled a PalmPilot out of his shirt pocket. "I'm ready."

Marina looked at him. "You're actually going to participate?"

"Right down to the organic seed we'll be throwing

at the happy couple when they head off on their honeymoon." He leaned forward and lowered his voice. "We don't use rice. The birds eat it and it's bad for them."

She opened her mouth, then closed it. "Someone's been spending a little too much time on the Internet."

"Internet, bridal magazines, whatever. When it comes to wedding planning, I'm your guy." A challenge brightened his dark eyes. "I'm in this all the way. Are you?"

If he thought he could scare her off, then he was in for a wild ride. "I'm in. And just for the record, I define stubborn."

"Me, too."

Ha! No way. He might think he was all that, but Marina was more than willing to take him on and win.

Julie sighed. "I thought you two might not get along, but I never considered this might become a competition. Listen. We're talking about a wedding. My wedding to Ryan. We need help, not a Las Vegas-style show. Bigger is not better. Don't be too creative. Let's just make it low-key and elegant, okay?"

Marina felt Todd's gaze shift to her. She stared right back at him and refused to be the first one to blink. "Julie, have I ever let you down?"

"No," Julie said slowly, as if she didn't want to admit it.

"So trust me."

Julie gave them each a copy of her list. Todd scanned his, then turned his attention back to Marina Nelson.

She was blond like her sisters, only her hair was

darker—more honey-gold. She was about an inch taller than Julie, with the same curvy build. They were obviously sisters and could almost have passed for twins. The main difference—aside from hair color—was the "I'm willing to take you on, big guy" attitude in the set of her chin. Julie was far more agreeable.

Todd had a rule when it came to women—why work hard? There were plenty of attractive females more than happy to come on to *him*. Some of it was due to his success as a businessman, some of it was his looks. Most of it was about the family fortune.

Whatever the reason, he rarely had to go searching for company. His romantic life was an ongoing series of short-term relationships with minimal commitment and effort on his part. That was how he liked things.

Marina was going to be anything but easy and he wasn't even trying to get her into bed. But Ryan had asked for his help, so he would put up with the overly verbal Nelson sister for the sake of his cousin.

He was even willing to admit—only to himself—that he was looking forward to taking her on. It had been a long time since a woman had done anything but let him get his way. Working with her would be good for his character, even if he did plan to win in the end.

"Basically we have the invitations done and that's it," Julie said as she studied her own copy of the list. "Grandma Ruth offered her house for the wedding and Ryan and I agreed it's an amazing place. But there are decisions to be made. It's a winter wedding. Do we want to risk the outside thing? It could be seventy-five or it could be raining."

"She mentioned something about a ballroom," Marina said. "On the third floor. Want us to check that out?"

"I've seen it." Todd kept his attention on Julie. "It would easily hold three or four hundred. A few less if you're interested in a sit-down dinner."

"We are," Julie said, making a note.

"But the guest list isn't nearly that big," Marina told him. "It's about a hundred."

"Ryan said it was closer to two hundred."

Marina turned to her sister. "That many?"

"It keeps growing."

"That's a lot of tables."

"I know. So I need you to check out the ballroom and see how it would be. Is there still room for dancing with all the tables in place? Where would the band go? I'm torn. Being outside would be great, but I'm not sure I can trust the weather, and I won't need to be stressed about one more thing."

"We'll decide that first," Marina said, taking notes. "That will affect all the other decisions. What's next?"

"Flowers, favors—nothing stupid, please—food, entertainment, a photographer and my dress. Oh, and you and Willow have to pick out bridesmaids' dresses."

Ryan was so going to owe him, Todd thought humorously. "Tuxes," he said.

Julie stared at him. "Oh God. You're right. The guys need tuxes."

"I'll take care of the dress myself," Marina said, smiling at him. "The dress is purely a girl thing."

"Do you plan to get a say in the tuxes?" he asked.

"Sure."

He waited while she began sputtering.

"Wait a minute," Marina said. "A bride's dress has to be something special. She's only going to get married once."

"I could say the same thing about Ryan. He'll want to look good and you don't trust me to make that happen. Why should I trust you?" Of course he had no real interest in the wedding gown, but fair was fair.

Julie waved her hand. "I don't care who goes to the bridal shop. Just find me an amazing dress. Nothing fitted at the waist, of course."

That's right, Todd thought. Julie was pregnant.

He knew Ryan was excited about being a father. While Todd never intended to marry, he liked the idea of having kids. The lack of wife would complicate things, but didn't make the situation impossible.

"I can't believe you want a say in the dress," Marina muttered.

He leaned toward her. "Think of all those models I've dated. Some of their fashion sense must have rubbed off on me."

"Did you talk about fashion much?"

"We didn't talk at all."

He heard her grind her teeth together and nearly laughed.

"Willow works for that nursery," Marina said as she ignored him. "I'll ask her for recommendations on the florist front."

"Good idea," Julie said.

"I know a photographer," Todd told her.

Marina widened her eyes. "Does he take pictures of people with or without clothes?"

"Both. You'll enjoy looking at her work."

"I don't care about naked," Julie said. "Does she do weddings?"

"They're her favorite."

"Good. Put her on the list. Marina, nothing too artistic. Just regular pictures."

"Gotcha."

They went over a few more things, then Julie left to find the dress pictures she'd torn out of magazines.

Todd turned his attention to Marina. "I think this is going to be fun."

"Oh, me, too."

"You don't like me much."

"I don't know you."

"You don't want to."

"Actually I haven't decided that. Amazingly enough, you haven't been on my mind at all."

One point for her side, he thought. "You didn't say nice things about me before. I heard you."

She tilted her head as she stared at him. "You have a reputation which, personally, I think you enjoy. But people form impressions based on that notoriety."

"You think I'm shallow."

"I don't think you've ever had to work very hard at anything but your company."

"Still, you agreed to go out with me. One date. You promised. Aunt Ruth told me."

Her gaze narrowed. "It seemed like a good idea at the time."

She might be uncomfortable with the idea of dating him, but he was the one who had to live with the reality of his aunt offering her granddaughters each a million dollars if one of them would marry him. It made him feel like a loser. What the hell was so wrong with him that a woman had to be paid that much money to make a commitment?

Not that he wanted to get married, but it was the principle of the thing.

Fortunately Julie and Willow were both out of the picture, which left only Marina. He would have refused even a single date with her, but Aunt Ruth had looked so happy at the thought and although he would rather face medieval torture than admit it to anyone, he was a sucker when it came to his aunt Ruth.

"It's only one date," he said. "What's the worst that could happen?"

"It will be three hours that will seem like a lifetime?" But there was a flash of humor in her eyes as she spoke.

"The wedding," he said. "We both have to be there, we're both in the wedding party, which means it wouldn't be much fun for anyone else we brought."

She nodded slowly. "We will have just spent all that time arranging the event, so we'll have plenty to talk about."

"We can have lots of champagne."

She grinned. "Always a plan. All right, Todd Aston the Third, I'll be your date for my sister's wedding."

Two

Grandma Ruth's three-story Bel Air mansion was just as awe-inspiring the second time Marina pulled in to the stone covered circular driveway. It was massive and out of place—this was Los Angeles, not eighteenth century England. But the rich lived different lives, Marina thought as she climbed out of her aging import. Lives with live-in staff. Her idea of help at home was a package of premoistened glass cleaning towelettes.

She glanced at the double door leading into the house and decided to wait until Todd showed up before going inside. Okay, sure, she shouldn't be intimidated by her grandmother's maid, but she was. So what? She had other positive attributes she could focus on.

Less than a minute later, a gleaming silver Mercedes

pulled into the driveway. The car was a sporty two-seater model, the kind that cost as much as the national debt of a small third world country.

The guy who climbed out of it was just as impressive. Tall, well tailored and sexy enough to encourage smart women to make some really stupid choices. She would have to make sure she didn't fall into the category. Fortunately he wasn't her type.

"Marina," Todd said with a grin. "I thought you would have already scouted the house and made the decision."

"We're a team, Todd. I totally respect that." Or she would as long as it suited her.

Speaking of suits, his was dark gray, with a subtle pattern in the weave of the fabric. His pale blue shirt contrasted with the deep burgundy tie. While she preferred a more casual look, he wore his power extremely well. She, on the other hand, looked like a college student with a limited budget. Although her skinny jeans had zipped up with no problem, which made this a very good day.

She collected her digital camera and a small notebook, then followed him to the front door. "I have about an hour," she said as she checked her watch. "Then I have to be back at UCLA for a class."

"What are you taking?"

"I'm not. I'm interpreting." She glanced at him. "I'm a sign language interpreter for deaf students. I specialize in chemistry and physics, mostly the upper division classes."

He raised his eyebrows. "Impressive."

"It's not that hard for me. I've taken all the classes

myself, so I understand the material. I have three advanced science degrees. Eventually I'm going to have to pick a Ph.D. program, but I'm not ready yet. I already knew how to sign, so I decided to do this for a couple of years."

His eyes widened. "*Three* advanced science degrees?"

She loved people underestimating her. "Uh-huh. It's less impressive when you know I started college at fifteen."

"Oh, sure. It's practically ordinary. You're pretty smart."

She smiled. "Smarter than you, big guy."

He laughed. "I'll remember that."

He knocked on the front door and when the maid answered, he greeted her by name.

"We're here to see the ballroom, Katie," he told the woman in uniform. "Then check out the backyard."

The maid nodded. "Yes, sir. Your grandmother told me you'd be stopping by. Would you like me to show you upstairs?"

"We can find it. Thanks."

Marina smiled at the other woman, then followed Todd across a huge foyer and up a wide, curving staircase.

"So how big is *your* staff?" she asked as they reached the second floor and walked along a long, carpeted hallway. There were dozens of paintings on the wall and pieces of furniture that were probably impressive antiques, if she knew anything about them.

"Five live-ins, six dailies."

"What?" she asked. She'd only seen his house from a distance—and it had been bigger than this one—but still. "What do they do?"

He turned to her, touched his finger to the tip of her

nose and smiled. "Gotcha. I have a housekeeper who hires people to keep the house clean and take care of the grounds. She comes in three days a week. I'd rather not have any staff, but the house is old and big and I'm not willing to deal with it, so she does."

Okay, one housekeeper *was* better than five live-ins.

They took a second staircase that flowed into a landing that was bigger than Marina's apartment. A wall of ornate doors opened into a ballroom the size of a football field.

She stepped into the center of the room and turned in a slow circle. There were gilded mirrors on the walls and dozens of sparkling chandeliers hanging from the ceiling. The parquet floor gleamed and reflected the sunlight from the windows.

The walls had been painted a neutral pale beige, so any color theme would work.

"We're talking about tables of either eight or ten," Todd said as he pulled out his PalmPilot and pushed a few buttons. "We can fit as many as thirty tables in here and still have room for people to get around."

Marina did the math. "Can we fit twenty-eight tables and still have room for dancing and the band?"

Todd looked at her. "Orchestra. Not band. Julie said elegant. Bands aren't elegant."

Maybe not, but she'd never been to a wedding with an orchestra. "You think the L.A. Philharmonic is available?"

He grinned. "I'd have to check their schedule, but I was thinking of something a little smaller. I have a group in mind that I've heard play at other venues."

Venues? So while the rest of America went to the

mall, the über rich had venues? "What sort of venues would these be?"

"Mostly fund-raisers. A couple of weddings. I'll find out where they're playing in the next couple of weeks and we'll go hear them. They're great. Trust me."

Trust him? Not yet.

She put down her notebook and began taking pictures of the vast space. "I really like this room," she said as she turned slowly to get every angle. "I'll e-mail these photos to Julie as soon as I'm done with class."

"There's more," he said and led her to a series of French doors. He unlocked the first one and opened it, then motioned for her to lead the way.

She stepped out onto a wide balcony that overlooked the property. Although if one couldn't see where the fence line was, did that make it an estate?

The grounds were stunning. She could see the terrace and the pool and the gardens beyond.

"This would give us extra space," he said as he joined her. "A place for people to get some air. We could put lights in the garden for the view."

"I like it," she said more to herself than him. "Anyone can get married in a backyard, but this is incredible. A once-in-a-lifetime opportunity."

She turned back to the ballroom where she could imagine the tables and guests and flowers. Talk about making some memories.

"So you prefer the ballroom?" he asked.

"I do, but it's Julie's choice. Let's go downstairs and take some pictures of the garden so she and Ryan can decide. Once we know which way they want to go, we're free to start making other arrangements."

They made their way back downstairs, then stepped out onto the manicured terrace. It looked more like the grounds of a five-star hotel than someone's home, she thought as she took pictures, not sure how she felt about her grandmother living here.

Something of her confusion must have showed because Todd asked, "What's wrong?"

She pocketed the digital camera and tucked her notebook under her arm. "I keep thinking how strange this is—that a grandmother I never knew about was alive and well about fifteen miles from where I grew up. That this is her world and I can remember times when we didn't have enough money to have meat with dinner."

She shook her head. "I'm not complaining. My mom was great and my sisters and I always had plenty of everything we needed. Money was tight, but that's how it was with most of our neighbors. I'm okay with that. But now, to find out there's a whole other way of looking at things, it's strange." She looked at him. "I'm not explaining myself well and this is more information than you wanted."

"Of course this is different. For what it's worth, Ruth regrets all the years she was apart from you and your family. Her husband, my uncle, was a hard man. He didn't believe in forgiveness. Ruth simply didn't have the strength to stand up to him."

"That's what she said."

"It's true."

Great. So it seemed she came from a long line of women who surrendered heart and mind to their men. All the more reason not to get involved.

He looked at her. "You should try to understand what Ruth went through."

Todd Aston the Third being sensitive? "Okay, now I'm freaked out on two different levels. The contrast between what I'm used to and this, and your emotional perception."

"I'm a man of great mystery."

That made her laugh. "Of course you are. Wealth, power and mystery. You should put that on your business cards."

He led the way around the side of the house toward their cars. "I'm way ahead of you, Marina. I have it tattooed on my back."

She grinned. "I thought you'd have a stick up your butt," she said before she could stop herself.

"They know how to fix that now. Isn't modern medicine a miracle?"

She sighed. "You know what I mean. I thought you'd be…different."

"Unpleasant?"

"Imperious."

"I can be, if that would make you happy."

"No, thanks." She opened her notebook. "Okay, venue research complete. Which leaves us with food, the cake, flowers, a photographer and all kinds of other messy details."

"The dress," he reminded her. "We'll have to look

at something off the rack. There's no time for a custom gown."

She glanced at him, surprised he would know that. "Let me guess. More bridal magazine research? Although somehow I can't see you sitting down with a latte and a bridal magazine."

"I can't have a latte then. Black coffee to combat all the girliness. It's about balance."

Until this moment, she hadn't thought of Todd as a person. At first he'd been just a name, then he'd been the guy who tried to break up her sister and Ryan. Then an annoyance who would get in her way about the wedding. But now...

"Why do you hide who you are behind your reputation?" she asked. "The money thing. The model thing."

He unlocked his car. "I've dated maybe three models in my life, Marina. You need to let go."

"You're right. I will."

"Good." He sat in his car and grinned. "Of course, two of them didn't speak English."

They didn't... Then how... She glared at him. "You had better be kidding. Not speak English?"

He nodded. "I was simply doing my part to improve American relationships with our neighbors." He smiled angelically. "I know a great caterer. I'll set something up and get back to you with the details."

With that he was gone.

Three days later Todd stood in front of the catering office and watched Marina walk toward him. She wore jeans, a UCLA sweatshirt and her hair pulled back in a ponytail. Not someone who dressed to impress.

There was also an air of determination about her that made him anticipate plenty of flying sparks. Planning a wedding might not be his idea of a good time, but so far Marina had been a pleasant surprise. Smart and sexy. He'd been looking forward to seeing her again.

When she stopped in front of him, she put her hands on her hips and glared at him.

"I looked you up on the Internet," she said. "The models in question spoke perfectly good English, albeit with an accent."

"Albeit?" he asked as he raised his eyebrows. "Are we in a Jane Austen novel?"

"What do you know about Jane Austen?"

"Every good useless male who only dates models knows all about chick flicks and Jane Austen. It's required. I not only saw *Bridget Jones's Diary* twice, I've seen the special features. Ask me anything."

She burst out laughing. The sound was light and sexy and made him want to touch her. All of her. Unexpected heat swept through him, startling him with its intensity.

He immediately took a step back, both physically and mentally. He and Marina were on a mission. He was here to protect Ryan's interests and not die of boredom in the process. If tweaking Marina's assumptions about him got him through the day, then he was up to the task. But actually enjoying her company—not a good idea. Getting involved with his aunt-by-marriage's youngest granddaughter wouldn't be very intelligent.

"This place comes highly recommended," he said as they made their way to the front door. "It's supposed to be good food with more choices than beef or chicken. If this is the one we pick, we'll be able to customize the menu. Or in our case, argue over food options."

"You think we're going to argue?" she asked.

"I'm counting on it."

"I'm a pretty agreeable person, but I'm sure you're difficult," she said as he held open the door. "I'll be flexible on food, but not the dessert thing."

"What dessert thing?"

She smiled at him. "That we have dessert. It's one of the great thrills of a wedding. You get dessert *and* cake. How often does that happen in life?"

"Far be it from me to get between a woman and her sugar fix."

"Pretty and smart," she murmured. "How impressive."

"I know." He turned his attention to the receptionist and introduced them.

"I'm Zoe," the woman said with a smile. "We're ready for you. If you'd come this way?"

They were led in to a small room set up like a dining area. The table for six had two place settings at one end.

Zoe seated them, then pointed out the menu printed on a single sheet by the plates.

"We'll go in order," she said. "We'll start with soups, then the salads and so on. Please make notes or write down any questions."

She left and then returned immediately with three small bowls for each of them.

"Lovely presentation," Marina said as she picked the sprig of garnish out of one of the bowls. "Why do they have to put some garden weed on top of a dish? What is it? How do we know where it's been?"

"The not knowing adds to the thrill of the moment."

She looked at him, her blue eyes wide. "Are you thrilled?"

She was close enough that he could see a couple of pale freckles on her nose and hint of a dimple in her cheek. Once again he thought about touching her…and didn't.

"Beyond words."

"Liar," she murmured, then took a taste of the first soup. "Split pea with something else. Not bad."

He tasted it and shook his head. "No, thanks."

They both passed on the creamy mystery soup, while he liked the chicken vegetable and Marina complained it was too healthy.

"We're at a wedding. Do we really have to get our five servings of fruits and vegetables in the first course?"

He poked around the bowl. "Not a lot of fruit that I can see."

"You know what I mean." She set down her spoon. "What about tortilla soup? Or a quesadilla? Doesn't that sound good?"

"You want Mexican food at your sister's wedding?"

Marina's shoulders slumped. "Not really, but I could go for some right now. I should have eaten before coming here. I'm really hungry."

"So you like food."

She narrowed her gaze. "Yes, some women eat. I

eat. Shocking, but true. I also run every day, so I can pretty much eat what I like and enjoy it. Do you have a problem with that?"

"Running with that chip on your shoulder must help with your workout. The extra weight would increase intensity."

She opened her mouth, then closed it. "You're saying I'm a little sensitive about the food thing?"

"Would I say that?"

"You're thinking I'm overreacting because you date models and I don't feel I measure up to their ideal."

"You're doing all the talking."

"I'm not intimidated. Mostly not. Sometimes, maybe a little. But I'd like to point out that these are my skinny jeans. They've fit all week and they look fabulous on me."

"Yes, they do." He'd admired the curve of her hips and her long legs when she'd first walked up. He was willing to take another look, if that would make her happy.

"I don't seek approval from anyone but myself."

"Why would you?"

She smiled. "You're humoring me."

"It seems safest. You have some attitude on you."

"I know. I don't get it. I'm actually a fairly calm person. I'm not sure what it is about you that pushes all my buttons."

"It's because I'm so smooth and handsome," he said as Zoe came in with several salad plates, along with a basket of rolls. "You're uncomfortable."

Marina waited until they were alone to respond. When Zoe had picked up the soup bowls and left, she said, "I'm not uncomfortable. You have an ego the size of Antarctica. You're not that special."

"Of course I am. You researched me. Who was the last guy you researched?"

"The men I know are totally normal. Researching is not required. You make me crazy."

"Then my work here is complete."

She shook her head. "Eat your salad."

He took a bite of the first salad. There were a lot of strange looking lettuces and shavings of things he didn't recognize. Salad was highly overrated, he thought grimly.

"Think about the guys you usually date," he said, enjoying the fact that he could get to her. "Scruffy, poor grad students. When compared to me, they don't have a chance."

She glared at him. "Oh, right. Why would dating the next brilliant man who will change the course of history by improving the world be considered interesting?"

He picked up a roll and leaned toward her. "They're nerds. They're not interesting yet and they're not good in bed. Admit it."

Fury darkened her eyes. She opened her mouth, probably to yell at him. He stuck the roll between her lips.

"Not bad," he said, pointing at the second salad. "I like the blue cheese. What do you think?"

She pulled the roll away and glared at him. "I think you're a pompous, egotistical ass."

He tasted the third salad and grimaced. "So you like me."

"I don't."

"Of course you do. But I was asking about the salads. What do you think?"

She pointed at the one he'd tasted third. "That one works."

He shook his head. "Not a good idea. There's too much garlic in the dressing."

"Since when do you know anything about cooking?"

"I don't." Could he help it that she set him up with one good line after the other? Sometimes a guy couldn't help cutting a break. "But I do know about weddings." He glanced around, then leaned toward her and lowered his voice. "Kissing. Lots and lots of kissing at weddings. You don't want the guests to have garlic breath."

Awareness crackled in the room. He thought Marina might get nervous or change the subject, but her gaze never left his. The humor was gone, replaced by a tension that quickly flared into need.

What would it be like to kiss her? What would her mouth feel like against his? How soft? How hungry? How sexy?

Was she the kind of woman who took charge, or did she like to be convinced? The possibilities were endless and suddenly he wanted to explore them all.

"I think you're overstating the problem," she said. "I don't think the garlic is that big a deal, but if it is, we could simply change the dressing on the salad."

"There's only one way to find out," he said and leaned in farther, then brushed his mouth against hers.

There was heat and need. They competed for his attention. Marina didn't move, but he heard her breath quicken. But before he could take things to the next level, Zoe returned.

"What did you… Oh. Sorry. Should I come back?"

Todd straightened. "No. We know what we need to do."

Three

Marina felt as if she'd been hit by a truck. Well, that wasn't right, she thought as she blinked to bring the room back into focus. Nothing bad had happened and she certainly wasn't squished. But she was out of breath and feeling a little two-dimensional all the same.

Talk about wow. The heat, the tingles, the need to jump Todd's bones and make him have his way with her. All from a teeny, tiny, innocent kiss. What would happen if he kissed her like he meant it?

A dangerous question, she told herself. Todd was nothing like she'd imagined. He was funny and charming. Too charming. She had to remember that any contact with a woman was just a game with him. That he had the emotional depth of a cookie sheet. She should enjoy the superficial attraction for the momentary pleasure and let the rest of it go. He didn't do relationships and she didn't do anything else.

Although technically she didn't do relationships, either. It was the whole fear thing. She didn't want to get lost in a man.

They sampled several entrées, which were okay and the desserts, which were great.

"Are you going to finish that?" she asked, eyeing his barely tasted dish of chocolate mousse.

Todd pushed the bowl toward her. "You're welcome to it."

She dipped her spoon into the creamy, foamy delight and then savored the burst of rich chocolate on her tongue. He watched her, his expression unreadable.

She wanted to think he found her passion for chocolate fascinating, but no doubt he was comparing her normal appetite to his dates' lack of appetite and finding her just a little odd.

"Finished?" he asked when she'd scraped the last of the pudding from the bowl.

She nodded and they walked out to the reception area. After collecting prices and a brochure from Zoe, they promised to be in touch within a couple of weeks, then left.

"What did you think?" Todd asked as they walked to their cars.

"It was good," she said, "but not dazzling. I want to be dazzled. I think the food should be spectacular, not just good."

He glanced at the price list. "Considering what

they're charging, I agree. So we still need a caterer. Do you have any suggestions?"

"I don't cater much, but I can ask around."

"I'll do the same. I'll also check with Ruth."

Ah, yes. Her grandmother. "She does the charity circuit," she said. "At least she's mentioned it. So she should be a great source of information." Marina frowned. "I wonder why she hasn't offered us advice."

"She promised not to meddle," Todd told her. "Don't get too excited—it's not going to last. She's a meddler by nature." There was a tone of affection in his voice.

"So you've forgiven her for coming to me and my sisters and offering each of us a million dollars if one of us were to marry you?"

He winced. "I'm working on it."

"Why?"

He shrugged. "She always had time for me and Ryan. Our parents took off for months at a time and left us behind. Aunt Ruth stepped into the void. When we were with her, it was like family."

Marina didn't know what to say to that. On the one hand, it explained Todd's fondness for his aunt. On the other, this was the same woman who turned her back on her own daughter.

"You're thinking about your mom," he said, surprising her.

"Yes. My mom was seventeen when she fell in love with my dad. That's pretty young. I can understand her parents being upset with her choice, but there are a lot of options between saying it's okay and kicking her out forever. How come they didn't try any of them?" She drew in a deep breath and let it go. "You're going to tell me it was because of Ruth's husband, Fraser. I've heard it all before. He was a difficult man who ruled his house and didn't give anyone second chances."

He was also the only father Marina's mother had ever known. Her biological father, Ruth's first husband, had died before Ruth had even realized she was pregnant.

"My mom was Ruth's only daughter," Marina said. "She should have tried harder. She should have made sure her daughter was all right."

Todd surprised her for maybe the third time in less than two hours when he put his hand on her shoulder and squeezed gently.

"You're right," he said quietly. "She stood by her husband instead of her daughter. Because of that, she spent the next thirty years regretting her decision, but being too afraid to do anything about it. That's got to be a hard way to live, for all of you. She'll never get back what she lost and neither will you."

She blinked at him. "That was really compassionate and understanding."

He scowled at her. "I am capable of rational and emotional thought."

"I know. I just didn't think you'd bother."

"That's flattering."

Now it was his turn to touch him. She grabbed his hand. "I'm sorry. That came out wrong. It's just the way you're presented in the local press and how people talk about you."

Maybe he wasn't a cookie sheet, she thought. Maybe he was actually a jelly roll pan.

The image made her smile, which made his scowl deepen. "You're really starting to tick me off," he muttered.

"I thought you said you had a well-developed sense of humor."

"I do. You're not being funny. Whatever you think about me, you're wrong."

She was beginning to think that might be a possibility.

He pulled out his trusty PalmPilot and pushed some buttons. "We still need a caterer, a photographer, flowers, a cake, a dress, tuxes. It's a long list."

"We'll get through it. I'll e-mail Julie the information on this place. At least we know we're having the wedding and reception in the ballroom. That's something."

"Lucky us."

She stared into his dark eyes and smiled. "Thanks for being so understanding about everything with my grandmother. It helps to talk about it."

"Yeah, yeah. I'll call you and we can set up our next taste testing."

Then he stunned her by bending down and kissing her. Only this kiss wasn't about garlic or proving anything. At least she didn't think it was. Instead it was quick, hot and bone-melting.

His hands rested on her shoulders, holding her in place. His mouth claimed hers with an expertise that made her more than willing to take this wherever he wanted to go. She lost herself in the pleasure of touch and lips and need.

He wasn't what she expected. *This* wasn't what she

expected. She found herself responding to him in ways she hadn't expected.

He tilted his head and brushed her lower lip with his tongue. She parted for him. He swept inside, teased into arousal, then pulled back and straightened.

"See you soon," he said.

What? He was leaving? He was going to kiss and run?

"But you... Why'd you..."

He smiled. "We were interrupted. I like to finish what I start."

To Marina_Nelson@mynetwork.LA.com
From Julie_Nelson@SGC.usa

I can't thank you enough. I really, really owe you for all your hard work. Thanks for taste-testing the first caterer and sorry it didn't work out. But you're right. I want fabulous food at the wedding and so does Ryan.

Interesting about the whole garlic/kissing thing. I hadn't thought that too much garlic could ever be a problem, but at a wedding? You're so right. So, did Todd demonstrate the perils of garlic kissing? ☺ Just kidding. I know he's not your type. Not earnest enough and yet lacking in character. But not totally awful. At least he's cute. Remember that when he starts to make you crazy.

We're having the best time. I can't wait to get more pictures and e-mails from you. Again, you're a total goddess for doing this!

Love and hugs, Julie

Marina opened the cardboard box and reached for the

tape dispenser. After sealing the bottom of the carton, she flipped it over and then looked at the bookshelves in the hallway.

"Does Julie really need to keep all these?" she asked, even though she already knew the answer.

Willow stuck her head out of the bedroom where she'd gone to tackle clothes. "Of course. They're books. She'll keep them forever."

"Does Ryan know what he's getting into? The whole pack rat thing?"

Willow grinned. "She's not a pack rat and yes, he knows exactly what he's getting into."

"Well, I didn't have a clue," Marina grumbled. "Between helping you pack Julie's place, you handling the renovations at their new place and me planning Julie's wedding, she is going to owe us big time. We're going to have to break our legs or something and force both of them to serve us."

"She'll be there every second of our recovery," Willow promised. She held out her left hand and pointed. "Would you hand that to me?"

Marina didn't turn to see the object in question. Instead she stared at her sister's ring finger—or more specifically, at the stunning diamond ring glinting there.

"You're engaged!" Marina yelled. "I'm so happy for you."

Willow laughed, then they were hugging and jumping up and down together.

"It's so beautiful," Marina said, grabbing her sister's hand and studying the impressive cushion-cut stone surrounded by baguettes. "When did this happen? You didn't say anything. How could you not blab the second you saw me?"

"It was hard," Willow admitted. "But I wanted a great reaction and you gave me one." She stared down at the ring. "As to the when, it was just last night. Kane and I had talked about getting married before, when he came to his senses and realized he loved me. But between then and now there hasn't been a word. I was willing to give him time to get used to the idea of just being in a serious relationship."

They moved into the living room and fell onto the sofa. Marina smiled at Willow's happy expression.

"Who would have thought that the strong silent type would turn out to be such a great guy," she said, thrilled that Kane had been the one in a million Willow deserved.

Her sister sighed. "I know. It's a miracle. He's incredible. Last night we were having dinner together. It was really romantic and there was music and suddenly he was on one knee and holding out the ring and saying he wanted to marry me and be with me forever." Tears filled her eyes. "I never thought my life could be so wonderful."

Marina hugged her again. "I'm happy for you. Beyond happy. Delighted. Giddy. There are other words I can't think of right now."

"I'm happy, too," Willow said.

Marina leaned against the cushion. "Two of my sisters getting married. I'll be the old maid aunt, a favorite of the children, but you adults will worry that I'm slowly slipping into madness."

Willow rolled her eyes. "Please. You're too smart for that. But I would say to be careful. Love is in the air and all that."

Marina shook her head. "I'm immune. Which is fine with me. I'm not looking to get married anytime soon."

"What about falling in love?"

"Maybe next year."

In truth, she liked the idea of falling for a guy. But along with the desire to be in love was a healthy dose of fear. Giving away her heart looked a little to much like giving away her sense of self. First Aunt Ruth, then her mother. Marina wasn't willing to be like either of them.

"So, another wedding," she said. "Have you two picked a date?"

"We're thinking spring. Well, after Julie's wedding, but before the baby's born."

"I can help with the planning. I'll be an expert."

"I would love that," Willow told her. "I wouldn't know where to start."

"Just ask me anything. Or Todd. He's actually pretty good at the whole wedding planning thing. Just don't tell him I said that."

Willow shifted so they were facing each other. "Really? He's not awful?"

"No," Marina said, still surprised by that bit of news. "He's actually nice. Funny, charming…I like him. I didn't expect that at all. I thought he'd be a jerk. I really didn't want to work with him on the wedding, but even though we don't agree on everything, I like having him help. It's a big responsibility and I like having someone to share in the process. Plus, he's fairly good-looking. Even if my day is going badly, it's fun to have a little eye candy to look forward to."

"I don't think he's the kind of guy who likes being called eye candy."

"Probably not, but we won't mention it."

Willow studied her. "So this is good?" she asked. "With Julie and Ryan getting married, Todd is kind of in the family now. We'll all be friends?"

"I think so. We'll mock his choice of women when he brings dates, but that will be entertaining."

"Something to look forward to," Willow said. "Todd's not the kind of guy to hang out by himself."

Marina nodded in agreement, but found herself wondering about the other women in Todd's life. No doubt he was seeing someone right now. Who was she? Some socialite or heiress? A high-powered businesswoman? Marina would guess that whoever she was, her wardrobe consisted of more than jeans and UCLA sweatshirts.

Not that she, Marina, was trying to impress him. They were working together on the wedding. Nothing more. Except he'd kissed her. She still couldn't seem to forget the flash of heat and need and desire that had nearly overwhelmed her. And that had been from a kind of nothing kiss. What would happen if he kissed her like he meant it?

"He's actually my date for the wedding," Marina

said. "We both promised Grandma Ruth we'd go on one date and the wedding seemed the easiest."

"Once again I encourage you to marry him so I can have a million-dollar nest egg," Willow said with a grin.

"Kane has money."

"Yes, but that's *his* money. A fortune of my own would be kind of fun."

Marina shook her head. "Sorry. I don't have any big plans to marry Todd. Not even for a million dollars."

"What about five million? I'll bet Grandma Ruth would be delighted to cough up a little more cash."

"Not interested."

Willow sighed. "I thought our sisterly love was supposed to be unconditional. I hate that it has limits."

"Life can be tragic."

Willow glanced back at her ring. "There are some bright spots. I have Kane."

"Yes, you do."

Willow looked at her. "You're next. Things happen in threes. First Julie, then me, so it's your turn."

"I don't think it works like that."

Not that she would say no to her own happily ever after, but there were complications. Falling for a guy meant trusting him completely. While she could see that happening, it also meant trusting herself, which she was a lot less sure about.

Four

Marina sat on the front stairs of her apartment waiting for Todd. As her watch ticked over to the exact minute he was due, his sleek, silver, expensive convertible rounded the corner and pulled up in front of her building.

She stood and sighed. "Pretty car," she said when he stepped out and walked toward her. "Very pretty car." Of course he looked good, too. The man knew how to wear a suit. But she didn't feel the need to share that.

He held out the keys. "Want to drive?"

She blinked. "Excuse me?"

"Drive. The. Car. You're supposed to be the smart one here. It shouldn't be such a complex concept. I've seen you drive. You know how."

She looked from him to the Mercedes and back. "But

it's your car. You're a guy. Guys don't share their cars. Certainly not really expensive ones like this."

"It's just a car, Marina. I buy what I like, but it's not my life." He shook the keys. "Now answer the question. Do you want to drive?"

She snatched the keys from him before he could change his mind. "Absolutely."

But as she made her way to the driver's side, she glanced at him. Sure, Todd had money and if something happened to this car, he could easily get another, but it was the principle of the matter. This wasn't normal behavior. Was he really so secure with himself that he could let her do this without a second thought?

She settled into the leather seat and surveyed the interior. There were the basics she was used to, along with a GPS display, dual zone air-conditioning and a sound system that looked complicated enough to be on the space shuttle.

"It's nice today," he said. "Want to put the top down?"

"Oh, yeah."

She scanned the controls and found the one that took care of the top, then put the key in the ignition and turned to watch the show.

It was a marvel of German engineering, she thought as the top automatically folded down and a built-in cover slipped over it. All without her doing anything.

Then she faced front, adjusted the mirrors, started the engine and prepared to be impressed.

"How fast can I go?" she asked.

"How much are you willing to pay for a ticket?"

"Good point. So where to?"

He pulled a piece of paper out of his shirt pocket. "Today we're taking care of table linens, place settings, tables and chairs, party favors and the tuxes." He glanced at his watch. "We have an appointment at the linen place, so let's go there first."

He gave her the address and she pulled out into the street. The car responded to her every instruction, the engine purred smoothly and she could feel the power hovering just a press of her foot away. The day was warm, the wind wiped her hair around and she felt pretty darned happy.

"I could get used to this," she said as she came to a stop at the light.

"So you're tempted by the dark side?"

She grinned. "More than tempted." Obviously a car like this wasn't possible on her budget, but maybe a used convertible wasn't out of the question. It could still be fun.

She drove to the rental place and resisted the urge to take an extra trip around the block, just for the driving pleasure. Instead she parked and climbed out.

"Thanks," she said, handing over the keys. "That was great."

"Anytime."

"As if you mean that. Still, I'm deeply impressed you let me drive it at all. You're very secure."

"I'm a macho kind of guy."

She laughed. "Not to mention modest. You're extremely modest."

They walked into the rental showroom.

"I called ahead," Todd told her. "They'll have tables set up for us. We can get some idea of what colors work well together and how formal or informal we want things to be."

She pulled her camera out of her purse. "I'm prepared to take pictures."

They walked into the showroom and saw nearly a dozen tables set for dinner. Each table was done in a different color, with coordinating china and a centerpiece.

They introduced themselves to the clerk there, who invited them to walk around and get ideas.

Marina immediately moved toward a round table with a pale pink tablecloth and elegant light yellow napkins.

The plates were cream, trimmed in silver; the centerpiece was a combination of pink and yellow flowers that trailed across the center of the table. Even seated, the guests would be able to see each other and the colors were warm and cheerful.

"I like this one," she said, only to realize she was talking to herself. Todd was across the room in front of a table done in deep reds and purples.

She winced as she got closer. The china was black, the napkins dark and the flowers looked like something out of a nightmare rather than appropriate for a wedding.

"It's elegant," he said when she paused next to him.

"It's scary. I don't think we're going to have many children attending, but what if the ones who did come were terrified?"

He glanced over his shoulder at the one she'd liked. "What if we didn't set the table for an Easter brunch?

Julie said low-key elegant. Bunnies and colored eggs don't fall into that category."

Marina looked at the table she'd loved. "Okay, maybe it's a little pale, but this is awful. I don't like the really tall centerpiece. You can't see the people across from you."

"Which could be a good thing if you didn't like them."

She smiled. "We can't guarantee that will be the case. What about that?"

She pointed to a table done in deep rose, with accents of green. The cream china provided a neutral backdrop for patterned salad and dessert plates. The centerpiece was more botanical than floral and it sat low enough to see over.

Todd studied the settings. "It's not fussy. That's good. The colors are a little girly, but the green's okay. I like the centerpiece."

"It's certainly different," Marina murmured as she got out her camera and started taking pictures. "Rose and green would be pretty colors, with cream sort of blending in."

She snapped pictures of the other tables, but concentrated on the one she and Todd agreed on. Then they went to the clerk at the front of the showroom and asked about a price list.

Todd held out the sheet so they could both see it. The charges were broken down by type of rental, as well as number of units needed. The more rented, the less the cost per item.

"We didn't talk about the glasses," she said.

"Honestly, I can't see Ryan caring. If it holds wine and champagne, he'll be good with it."

"You're not going to argue on general principle?"

"Only to keep things interesting."

They were standing close together. Close enough for their arms to brush. Marina was aware of how much taller Todd was than her and how the heat from his body made her just a tiny bit squishy inside.

She did *not* want to be attracted to Todd, she reminded herself. It was that stupid kiss. If that hadn't happened, she never would have thought of him as more than just Ryan's friend and someone she had to learn to deal with for the next few weeks. He wouldn't have been…a man.

She forced her mind to focus on the project at hand. "Look, they can recommend a florist," she said. "That's good. We need more recommendations. The chair rental isn't too bad. We're going to need chair covers, though."

He swore softly. "They're four bucks each. With two hundred chairs, that's eight hundred dollars to throw a piece of cloth over the chair? Can't they be naked?"

She patted his arm. "No. They look better covered."

"Ryan and I are in the wrong business. If you rent out those covers twice every weekend, even with the cost of the initial purchase and cleaning, you're still raking in the money."

"So invest in the bridal business."

He looked around and shook his head. "It's too emotional. Give me a good high-tech start-up any day."

"But you could expand. Diversify."

"Maybe." He sounded doubtful.

She looked up at him. "So how did you get started?

Do you wake up one morning and think 'Hey, let's be venture capitalists'?"

"Not exactly. Ryan and I had a buddy back in college. He had a great idea for software, but he didn't have the money to manufacture or market it. We decided to finance his business."

"So you used your allowance money for the week?"

He shook his head. "Trust fund money."

"Oh, of course," she said knowingly. "That's where I go when I'm short on cash. It's so handy having that spare billion or two to fall back on."

"You enjoy mocking me, don't you?"

"It's pretty fun."

He folded the price sheet and handed it to her. "The company took off. By the time we graduated, Ryan and I had made our first million."

Impressive, she thought, but she wasn't going to say that to him. "Does the silver spoon ever choke you?" she asked.

He ignored her. "We both paid back out trust funds with interest and never had to tap into it again. Our company has been profitable ever since."

So except for his start-up cash, he'd earned his fortune the old-fashioned way. She would never have guessed. "Make any mistakes?"

"A few. Fortunately they didn't cost too much. Not every new company is going to make it and all the experts in the world can still be wrong. But we have good instincts."

And money, she thought. "No wonder you're considered a hot bachelor. How is it you've survived all this time without being trapped by some determined young woman?"

He smiled, but his eyes were cold and distant. "I've been burned enough times to not trust anyone."

"That can't be fun," she said, wondering if they had the same problem for different reasons. "How can you get close if you don't trust?"

"I don't need to get close to get what I want."

Which made sense, she thought, but was also sad. "That's got to get lonely."

"You don't have a guy in your life. Are you lonely?"

"No." Not exactly. Sometimes she wanted more, but the price of that always scared her away.

"So we're not so different," he said.

"Except for the millions and the fact that you date models, we're practically twins separated at birth."

"You're never going to let the model thing go, are you?"

"Um…not really."

The tux shop was well lit and elegant. Not exactly like those places at the mall. Marina felt distinctly underdressed, especially when the salesperson, a gorgeous brunette in her mid-twenties, stepped out from behind the counter in an outfit that looked as if it cost as much as Marina's rent.

"May I help you?" she asked, her gaze locking on Todd.

"We're here to look at tuxes," he said. "For a wedding."

The woman—Roxanne, according to her nametag—sighed. "Yours?"

"No. I'm the best man. The groom is out of the country. I'm supposed to make the right decision without him."

"I see." Roxanne turned her piercing green gaze on Marina. "And you are?"

"The sister of the bride. I get a vote."

"Wonderful."

Roxanne's attention swung back to Todd. Marina had a feeling it was never going to stray again.

"We have an amazing collection of designer tuxedos," Roxanne said, her voice low and sultry. "They're available for rent or purchase. Does the groom have your build?"

Todd glanced down at himself, then at Marina. "We're about the same size, don't you think?"

Marina nodded. "Pretty much. We want something simple, but elegant. Unfortunately the colors haven't been picked yet, so we're not ready to place the order."

Roxanne continued to gaze at Todd. "That's fine. You can try on whatever you like to see what makes you happy, then come back later."

Marina had a feeling Todd could visit every day and Roxanne wouldn't mind.

The three of them walked over to the display rack of tuxedos. Roxanne eyed Todd's body in a way that made Marina feel that she had stumbled into something intimate, then pulled out several selections.

"There are color choices, of course," Roxanne said. "Traditional black, various shades of gray, a few in other colors such as dark blue."

Todd grimaced. "Black or gray works for me. We're just looking for a regular tux. Bow tie and cummerbund."

"I like vests better," Marina said. Todd looked at her, Roxanne didn't.

"Vests?" He sounded doubtful. "I never wear a vest."

"How often do you put on a tux? Cummerbunds remind me of a high school prom. A vest can be elegant."

He shrugged. "Okay, but then I want a regular tie. A vest with a bow tie makes me feel like a grandfather."

Roxanne ran her hand down his arm. "You're certainly not that, are you?"

Marina held in a gagging noise. "At least try on both," she suggested. "If you hate it when it's on, then you can whine to Ryan."

"I don't whine."

"Oh, please. I've heard you."

Roxanne moved between them. "Let me get your size," she said, whipping a tape measure out of the jacket pocket of her very tailored and body-hugging suit. "Just hold your hands at your sides and relax."

Marina leaned against the counter as Roxanne did a very *thorough* job of the measuring. There was so much touching and cooing that even Todd started to look uncomfortable.

"All right," Roxanne said when she finally finished. "Let's get you into a dressing room and see how things go."

As she went into the back to get the samples, Marina grinned. "I hope she's quiet, because I embarrass easily. If the two of you start moaning, I'm out of here. Oh, give me the car keys so I can abandon you."

Todd gripped her arm. "You're not going anywhere. That woman scares me."

She laughed. "Oh, please. Is the big, bad millionaire frightened by the little girl in the tux shop? Poor Todd."

He narrowed his gaze. "You think this is funny."

"It kind of is."

It would be different if she were in a relationship with him. Then Roxanne's act would be a little disconcerting. But as it was, she could just have lots and lots of fun at his expense.

There was a tiny twinge of something buried inside her stomach, but she wasn't going to worry about whatever stray feeling she might have. It wasn't jealousy. It couldn't be. This was Todd. Someone she could never in a million years care about.

He pulled her into the dressing area with him. "Who's laughing now?" he asked as he jerked open a slatted door leading to a big dressing area, complete with a wooden chair. "Have a seat."

She folded her arms over her chest. "Excuse me? I can't sit here and watch you undress." Her cheeks got hot just from her thinking about it. She lowered her voice. "I barely know you."

"I'm wearing briefs," he said. "What's the problem? Pretend we're at the beach. I'm not going to be left alone with that woman."

He was serious. She wasn't sure if she was shocked or about to break out in hysterical laughter. "You expect me to protect you?"

"Damned straight."

She couldn't figure out what he wanted from her. Did he want her to act like she was jealous? Was this his ego talking? Did he need every woman on the planet panting for him so that he could sleep at night? Or was it something else? Was he seriously uncomfortable?

While she wanted to believe the best of him, his reputation made it impossible. So he was playing her.

Fine. She could play, too. She could make him sorry he'd ever pulled her into his game.

She walked to the edge of the platform and grabbed a handful of his jacket, then tugged until he stepped down onto the carpeted floor. Then she raised herself up on tiptoe, wrapped one arm around his neck and pressed her mouth to his.

She was determined this should be a whole lot more than that brief kiss they'd shared before. She wanted to teach him a lesson. So she kept her lips slightly parted and pressed against him as if she meant it.

After a brief second of shocked stillness, Todd put both his arms around her, hauled her closer and kissed her back. He brushed her lips with his, then took advantage of her invitation and swept inside.

He moved purposefully, a man on a mission. He tasted faintly of coffee and mint—and he knew how to kiss.

The second his tongue touched hers, passion exploded. The feeling was so intense, she half expected the building to shake. There was so much heat and need and pleasure in the way he explored her mouth, teasing, king, retreating, returning.

Wanting blindsided her. She couldn't think, so she

She felt her lips begin to twitch, but she managed to hold in her grin. "All right. If it's that important to you. I'll sit here and watch you try on clothes. But I have to tell you, I'm a little disappointed. I thought you'd be better with women than this. It's another hope dashed. Any more disappointments like this and I'll need therapy."

He glared at her. "I know her type. She's not going to take no for an answer."

"And the big, bad millionaire doesn't want to hurt her feelings," Marina said, mocking him with a baby voice.

His eyes narrowed, but before he could respond, Roxanne appeared with several tuxedos. She came to a stop when she saw Marina in the dressing area.

"You're helping?" she asked in a voice that indicated such a thing could not be possible.

"Absolutely," Todd told her. "Marina has perfect taste."

"He's pretty helpless without me," Marina said with a smile. "Practically unstable."

Todd's gaze lasered in on her face and she had a feeling she might have to pay for that later, but who cared? This was a side of him she could never have imagined and she planned to enjoy every minute of it.

Not only seeing him as someone with flaws and weakness, she thought as Roxanne hung the tuxes on a hook and flounced out of the room, but as someone who was a lot more interesting than she'd first realized.

It wasn't until he pulled off his tie and began to unbutton his shirt that she realized the small detail she'd overlooked. The dressing room was oversized, but still relatively close quarters considering she and Todd hadn't known each other very long and he was about to take his clothes off in front of her.

He'd said to pretend they were at the beach. In theory, briefs wouldn't show any more than swim trunks, but they *weren't* at the beach and a really good-looking guy was undressing. Where was she supposed to look? Or not look?

He shrugged out of the shirt. His broad chest was well muscled and defined. She liked the faint dusting of hair that trailed down to his waistband. But when he reached for that waistband, she found herself suddenly staring at the floor.

"Ryan had better appreciate this," Todd muttered.

"You'll figure out a way to make him pay," she said, noting his socks were dark and looked new.

There was a rustle of movement, then he pulled on the pants from the first tux. Safety at last.

She decided to distract herself from the process by being busy. After handing him his shirt, she slipped the jacket off the hanger and studied the weave of the fabric, then fingered the lapel.

Roxanne appeared in the doorway. "Vest or cummerbund?" she asked, holding out one of each.

"Vest," Marina said, taking it from her and handing it to Todd. "You said you'd try."

He grunted, then slipped it on. Marina admired the way the cut emphasized the breadth of his shoulders and the narrowness of his hips. A faint tingle quivered to life somewhere behind her belly button.

He took a tie from Roxanne and eased it under his collar. After securing the knot, he put on the jacket.

"There's a three-way mirror out here," Roxanne sai

He followed her into the large center area of th dressing rooms. He stepped onto the platform in fro of the mirror and stared at his reflection.

"What do you think?" he asked.

"Magnificent," Roxanne purred as she stepped u behind him and began smoothing down the shoulder and pulling at the hem of the jacket.

Marina agreed with the sentiment, even as the othe woman's need to touch every inch of Todd got on he nerves. This was a business, not a petting zoo.

Determined to be mature and let Todd handle th situation, she ignored Roxanne and her roving hands.

"I like the vest," she said.

Todd nodded. "Me, too. I see what you're going f It's less traditional than the cummerbund, but it lo great. We can't order anything until Julie and Ryan colors, but we can give them a few ideas."

"We have a Web site," Roxanne said, leaning his ear and pressing her breasts into his back. "I' down the item number so your friend can go o see which tux you're talking about. If he loo good as you in this, it's going to be some w

Marina held in a groan as Todd sidesteppe "Great. Why don't you go get that inform

She reluctantly stepped back. When dressing room, he turned to Marina.

"You're supposed to be protecting n

"You're big enough to protect your

"We're supposed to be a team. I'd r

reacted instead. She tilted her head and kissed him back. When he moved his hands up and down her back, she explored his shoulders, then his arms. He was all honed muscle and warmth. One of his hands got tangled in her long hair. He tugged slightly, pulling her head back. She let him have his way and was rewarded when he kissed his way down her neck.

The soft, hungry, openmouthed kisses made her want to whimper. Her entire body clenched as her breasts swelled in anticipation. She wanted to be on her back, on any flat surface. She wanted him between her legs, taking her hard and fast and damn the consequences.

That thought—one she'd never had before in her life—stunned her. She pulled back just as she heard the sound of a very irritated person clearing her throat. She turned and saw Roxanne standing in the entrance to the dressing room.

"You two should get a room," the saleswoman said, her voice icy.

"Interesting thought," Todd drawled.

Roxanne turned and left.

Marina stood there, not sure what to think let alone what she should say. Talk about unexpected passion. And awkward.

Several comments floated to the surface of her brain, but they all sounded stupid. Even if they didn't, she wasn't sure she could speak. Her throat was dry and tight and she had a bad feeling her voice would sound breathless.

"Marina," Todd began.

She held up a hand to stop him, then swallowed and forced herself to look at him.

Big mistake, she thought when she saw the hunger in his dark eyes. Her gaze zeroed in on his mouth…a mouth that could obviously drive a woman wild wherever it kissed her.

"I was teaching you a lesson," she said, her voice shaking a little. "At least I was supposed to."

"You're not what I expected, either."

Was that good or bad?

"You're not my type," she continued. "I want to plan my sister's wedding. Nothing else."

She met his gaze. Some of the hunger had faded, but there was just enough there to make her want to throw herself at him and do it all again.

"I agree," he said.

It took her a second to realize he was responding to what she said, not what she'd thought.

"So this never happened," she told him. "Nothing happened."

"Something happened. But we can ignore it—if you prefer."

Which was as close to a good answer as she was going to get, she thought. She left him alone to change back into his street clothes and walked out to wait by the car.

It wasn't the fact that she'd enjoyed the kiss that bothered her. It was that she'd been willing to give herself to him without knowing him. Without deep feelings. Her level of passion scared her.

Todd was a lot more interesting than she'd ever

imagined. Liking him was a surprise. Wanting him, equally startling but there it was. But the two together? No way. They made the situation more than danger-ous—they made it deadly.

She couldn't afford to fall for someone like him. If she did, she would be destroyed. She'd seen it happen. She knew what it cost.

To Marina_Nelson@mynetwork.LA.com
From Julie_Nelson@SGC.usa

What do you mean you kissed Todd! You can't just e-mail "oh by the way, I kissed Todd today" and then hit send. It's wrong on so many levels. You kissed him? On the mouth?

Why? That's so not like you. It's not about the million dollars is it? Please say it isn't. That's not like you, either. Todd? Seriously? How was it? Wait. I'm not sure I want to know.

He's nothing like your type. You always fall for sweet, nerdy guys who are going to save the world. Not powerhouse alpha males with attitude. He dated models. You remember that, right? Are you okay?

On a completely different topic, we love the sage/rose combination for our colors. Go with that, but nothing too matchy-matchy, please.

To Julie_Nelson@SGC.usa
From Marina_Nelson@mynetwork.LA.com

I'm fine. Totally fine. The kiss just kind of hap-pened. It's a long story and I thought he was playing me, so I kissed him. It doesn't mean anything. I wouldn't have mentioned it except I thought maybe he'd say something to Ryan and then Ryan would say something to you and then you'd be mad because I didn't tell you myself. That's all. Although now that I think about it, Todd isn't the type to brag.

As to the kiss, it was just a kiss, you know? Nice. I know he's not my type. You have nothing to worry about.

I'm glad you picked colors. That will help with the planning. I love the rose/green combo, too. And I swear, nothing that matches in a cute way. We'll go for shades and variations on a theme. It's going to be fabulous.

To Marina_Nelson@mynetwork.LA.com
From Julie_Nelson@SGC.usa
OHMYGOD!! You already know what type Todd is? What else do you know that you're not telling me? What else is happening there? You'd better not fall for him, Julie. I mean it. I'm thousands of miles away and I'd miss everything.

To Julie_Nelson@SGC.usa
From Marina_Nelson@mynetwork.LA.com
LOL. Don't sweat it. I'm not falling for Todd in any way. You have nothing to worry about.

Five

Todd drove slowly through the traffic around UCLA, then pulled over to the curb. He scanned the crowd of students, then saw Marina talking to a young woman.

Not talking, he reminded himself. Signing.

The two women faced each other, their hands moving in a graceful dance he couldn't decipher. Marina nodded, then glanced over her shoulder. She saw him and waved, then pointed at the car and signed something to her friend. The friend nodded, they hugged, then Marina started toward him.

He watched her walk. In her jeans and long-sleeved T-shirt, she fit in with the other students around her. He let his gaze linger on her swaying hips, then moved his attention to the way her long golden hair fluttered. She looked like a commercial for some sexy product. Buy whatever it was and get a girl like this.

She opened the passenger side door and slid inside. "Hey," she said. "Going to let me drive again?"

"No. Too much power will go to your head."

"So typical," she muttered as she fastened her seat belt. "Why do men feel they have to hold out on women? Don't give the poor females too much responsibility or power. They won't be able to handle it."

"Women control the majority of wealth in this country."

"A fact that makes me smile every time I hear it. I know you don't want me driving because my skill level threatens your masculinity."

"Not for long. I'm in therapy."

She laughed and he joined in. Their last meeting had been at the tux shop, where she'd kissed the hell out of him and had left him wanting more. He hadn't yet decided what, if anything, he was going to do about that wanting. For now it was enough to simply enjoy Marina's company.

As he pulled back into the traffic, he tried to remember the last time he'd wanted to just be with a woman. To hang out and talk and tease without counting the minutes until he could get her into bed.

It wasn't that he didn't want to sleep with Marina— he did. But he also liked her.

When was the last time that had happened? Liking. He'd almost forgotten how that felt. Not that he trusted her. He trusted no woman. But he'd been looking forward to being with her today ever since the last time he'd seen her.

"How did you get interested in sign language?" he asked.

She glanced at him. "I'm embarrassed to admit I first learned because one of my girlfriends had a hunky older brother who was deaf. I was about fourteen at the time. He was older and brooding and I knew that inside he was really deep and fascinating and that he would fall madly in love with me if only we could communicate. I took a beginning sign language class and really enjoyed it, so I kept going."

"What happened with the guy?"

"He turned out to be a total jerk who just happened to be deaf. Still, I'm grateful he put me on this path. I became a certified interpreter. It was a great part-time job for me through college."

She glanced at her watch. "I'm sorry I have to split up our day."

"No problem."

"It's an important class. So I appreciate you being flexible."

"Far be it from me to stand in the way of someone's education."

"Spoken like a true member of the elite."

They were heading over to a different caterer to sample food, then meeting up later at his place to interview a florist.

"Now that Ryan and Julie have picked their colors, we can make some firm decisions," he said. "I let the florist know what the colors were and she'll bring appropriate samples."

"Good. I think the rose-green combo gives us lots of room and areas of compromise. The boy stuff can be green, the girl stuff pink."

"Then everyone's happy."

"Exactly." She smiled at him.

He braked for the stoplight and smiled back. While they were looking at each other he said, "That was some kiss the other day."

Instantly her eyes widened and color stained her cheeks. She jerked her gaze away from him and stared out the windshield. "Yes, well, you said you needed protecting."

He'd wondered what she'd thought about their kiss. Had it been as powerfully erotic for her as it had been for him? Now he knew the answer to that was yes. He also knew she was a little embarrassed and wondered why.

"Not that I thought you really needed protecting," she said, still not looking at him. "You can handle women like that in your sleep."

"I'm more interesting when I'm awake." He drove through the intersection. "I wasn't expecting the passion."

"Just because I'm smart and into science doesn't meant I'm not like other people."

"You're not like other people, but that's a good thing. I'm not complaining, Marina. I like who you are."

"Oh. Good. Not that your opinion matters."

"Of course not."

She glanced at him. "It *was* a pretty hot kiss."

"I agree. I might need to be rescued later."

"I don't think so. You can save yourself without help from me."

"That's kind of cold."

"Live with it."

He chuckled and she smiled. Then she started talking about what Julie had said about the place settings. But most of his attention was on another, more interesting topic. Namely the idea of getting Marina into his bed.

He wanted her. That wasn't the question. He knew they would be great together. He'd learned that the first real kiss told a hell of a lot about chemistry and compatibility and desire. He and Marina had it all times ten. But sleeping together wasn't exactly intelligent.

For one thing, they would be connected to each other for the rest of their lives. Between his aunt by marriage being her grandmother and her sister marrying his cousin, they were in each other's worlds. Having sex would only make a complicated situation more awkward.

For another thing, she wasn't his usual type. She didn't play when it came to men and he didn't believe in getting serious when it came to woman. Better to keep things simple.

But it had been a great kiss. Thinking about it had kept him up much of the last couple of nights and that hadn't happened to him…ever.

Marina stared down at the small plate of pasta in front of her. While she appreciated the artful presentation, she was starting to get a little paranoid.

She leaned closer to Todd and whispered, "Is it just

me, or has every dish been covered with some kind of cream sauce?"

"It's not you," he whispered back. "The salad dressing, that creamy soup, the chicken, the crab cakes."

"Now this pasta," she murmured. "If we picked this place, we'd have to have white as our accent color."

She raked her fork through the perfectly cooked fettuccini. She couldn't complain about the food itself. The shrimp were delicate, the diced vegetables crisp, the sauce a decadent blend of cream and cheese and whatever spices went into it, but still.

"We can leave," he told her.

"Do you hate the food?" she asked.

"No. It's good. It's just…"

"Too much?"

He nodded. "Exactly."

A few minutes later, the dessert samples arrived. Marina managed to hold it together while the hostess explained what each dish was, then began to giggle when the women returned to the kitchen.

Todd raised his eyebrows. "Which will it be? The molten chocolate cake in cream sauce? The berries with cream sauce? The bread pudding with a chocolate cream sauce or the selection of sorbets with a ginger-cream topping?"

She took a bite of the bread pudding. "It's delicious," she said. "Really fabulous."

"I like the food," he said, sounding doubtful.

"I do, too. It's just so rich. My stomach already feels funny. Maybe the owner was a cow in a previous life and all this cream sauce is a way to get back to her roots."

Todd stared at her. "That's odd, even for you."

"I'm searching for an explanation. Okay, I'll e-mail Julie and tell her the food is amazing, but it's cream sauce central. Then they can decide."

They stood. She put her hand on top of her stomach. "Can we stop at a mini market on our way back? I'm dying for a soda to wash away the cream sauce flavor."

"Right there with you."

After her class, Marina drove to Todd's place to meet with the florist. Although she'd been to the gatehouse in back a few months before, she'd never seen the main house up close until today.

As she drove through the open wrought-iron gates, she stared up at the giant four-story mansion. There were dozens of windows and actual gables.

"And I thought Grandma Ruth's place was impressive," she muttered.

The grounds were manicured and endless. When she parked in front of the house, her car looked like a toy that had been left out by a careless child.

Sure, she'd known that the rich were different and that Todd was rich, but until this moment, she'd never realized exactly how rich. She had a bad feeling they were talking billions.

She headed up to the wide double doors, then paused as she glanced down at her jeans. Should she have dressed for the occasion?

Just then the front door opened and Todd stood there. "Take it all in?" he asked.

"Not yet. Do you give tours on alternate Wednesdays?"

"Only for a select few. Come on."

He'd changed out of his suit and was also dressed in jeans and a long sleeved shirt, which should have made her more comfortable. But he looked too good—all hard muscles and sleek sexy male. So between his butt and the elegance of the house, she didn't know where to look first.

She walked onto a marble entry floor and resisted the impulse to step out of her shoes. The foyer was large and oval, with a baby grand piano by the staircase. Right. Because every decent foyer *should* have room for a piano. There were incredible pieces of furniture that were probably antiques and paintings that looked both real and important.

Todd closed the door behind her. "What are you thinking?"

"I'm wondering how many bedrooms."

"More than ten."

"Okay. Good. So do you rent out to large families or simply invite small countries to move in?"

"It depends on my cash flow for the month."

He was joking, but there was something about his expression. Something almost…wary.

"Am I reacting wrong?" she asked. "Should I pretend I'm not impressed and a little intimidated?"

"It's just a house."

She laughed. "It's a really big house and you live here by yourself. That's a little strange."

"I grew up here. It's big and expensive to keep up, but it's been in my family for three generations and now it's my responsibility."

She looked around at the massive chandelier and the fresh flowers. "It's like a really great hotel. Show me the fluffy robe and the room service menu and I'll move in."

"We don't have room service."

She sighed. "Then forget it. Room service is a deal breaker for me." She looked at him. "How do they usually react? The other women?"

"They start by calculating how big a settlement they'll get when the marriage ends."

"Ouch. Not everyone you've dated has been in it for the money. A few of them must have actually liked you."

He chuckled. "You're not very good for my ego. Many of the women I date actually like me. The money is just a big plus." He put an arm around her shoulders and led the way through an arched doorway. "I don't usually show them the house."

"I wouldn't. Not until you're fairly serious. The ones who are in it for money won't be able to pretend anymore and the ones who are will be scared to death."

"*You're* not scared."

They were close enough that she could feel the heat of his body, which made her remember how it had been to be in his arms. How he'd pulled her close and kissed her back and made her tingle all over.

"We're not dating," she reminded him. As far as she was concerned, they never would. Todd was too dangerous for her peace of mind. She wouldn't have thought she could be scared by a guy, but in some ways he would never know about, he terrified her.

If only he didn't turn her on. Reluctantly she stepped free of his embrace.

They stopped in a large family room. There were two sectionals, a couple of armoires, side tables, a writing desk and nothing about the room felt crowded.

"Nice," she said, appreciating the warm colors and overall comfort of the space. "You have a decorator."

"Of course. I'm a typical guy. If it were up to me, the entire world would be beige."

Somewhere in the distance, she heard the sound of chimes.

"The doorbell," he said. "Probably the florist. Have a seat and I'll let her in."

She crossed to one of the sectionals and sat down. To her right was a drinks cart made of incredibly beautiful inlaid wood. Instead of liquor, there were an assortment of soft drinks, along with ice, flavored water and a few snacks.

"Somewhere a housekeeper or cook is lurking," she murmured to herself as she put ice in a glass and popped the can of her favorite soda. There was no way Todd had put this together himself.

What must it be like to grow up in a place like this? She couldn't begin to imagine. While the house was something out of a movie, she had a feeling it might not have felt very comfortable for a kid. Todd was an only child. This was the kind of house that screamed out for bunches of kids. Had he ever been lonely?

Todd returned with a tiny woman of indeterminate age. He was laden down with armfuls of books and portfolios. She had two baskets with dozens of flowers in them.

"Marina, this is Beatrice. Beatrice, Marina is the bride's sister."

"How lovely that the two of you are planning the wedding together," the other woman said with a smile. She glanced around at the furniture and turned to Todd. "Perhaps some kind of dining room would be better suited?"

"Sure. Right this way."

"Can I get you something to drink first?" Marina asked.

Beatrice glanced at the cart. "Water, please, dear. Bottled if you have it."

Marina filled a second glass with ice, grabbed a bottle of water and trailed after them. As they moved from the family room to the dining room, she braced herself to be both impressed and intimidated.

Good thing, too, because the dining room could easily seat thirty, although the table was currently set with only a dozen chairs. Still, by the way it sat in the center of the room and the number of thick legs clustered together, she would guess there were about eight or ten leaves that fit into it.

Two hutches flanked leaded glass windows, while a long buffet sat in the center of the opposite wall. There were four chandeliers and a fireplace.

Todd set the books on the table, while Beatrice began to lay out dozens of flowers.

"I understand the bride and groom have chosen their

colors," she said as she clustered various blooms together. "That's always helpful. Rose and green will be lovely. However, I have some ideas for something a little different. A twist on the ordinary. For example, here we have dusty-rose colored tulips with green gladiolus. Not traditional, but they look beautiful."

Marina wasn't into plants or flowers, but as she knew what tulips looked like, she could figure out the gladiolus by default. The green petals were amazingly lush and the color was perfect next to the deep pink of the tulips.

"They're gorgeous," she murmured, then looked at Todd. "What do you think?"

"Nice."

She smiled. "Too much girly stuff?"

"I'm not into flowers. This seems fine."

Beatrice pulled out a spiny looking display. "Here we have bromeliad, ginger and anthurium. Again, not traditional, but the colors are perfect and these arrangement could make a charming table."

She handed Marina a ball of flowers in a yellowish shade of green. "Chrysanthemum balls. Very elegant. This sort of thing can be hung from the back of chairs." She thrust a handful of green berries at Todd. "Hypericum berries. A perfect green."

She brought out more and more flowers until Marina couldn't hold anymore. Todd was equally laden down.

Then Beatrice turned to the books. "I have pictures from various weddings. We'll look at them now."

She flipped through dozens of photos, explaining the different flower possibilities.

"You said there would be a separate room for the ceremony?" she asked.

Marina nodded. "There's a perfect room off the main ballroom. We'll set it up with rows of seating, so that space will need flowers, as well."

Beatrice began to talk about what they could do, but suddenly Marina found it difficult to listen. She felt hot and flushed, although at the same time, she felt a chill. Her stomach had taken a turn for the uncomfortable, as well. It seemed to flip over on itself in a way that made her want to gag.

Cautiously she put down the flowers. She'd never been allergic to anything before, but maybe the overdose of pollen was getting to her.

Todd looked at her. "Are you all right?"

Her stomach gave another lurch and she had a bad feeling she was about to throw up.

"Not really," she said, interrupting Beatrice midexplanation. "Is there a bathroom nearby?"

"Sure." He put down his armful of flowers. "I'll be right back," he told the florist and led Marina out of the room.

Down a very elegant hall she was in no shape to appreciate, was a spacious guest bath.

"It's my stomach," she said. "I don't know what's wrong."

"Don't worry about it. I'll handle Beatrice."

Despite the suddenly twisting sensation in her stomach, she managed a smile. "I don't think anyone can handle Beatrice, but you go ahead and try."

"Come out when you feel better."

"Sure. I'll probably just be a minute."

She closed the bathroom door behind her and two seconds later lunged for the toilet.

Marina had no idea how much time had passed. She'd already thrown up twice and had a bad feeling she wasn't done. She felt shaky and weak, hot and cold, and a distinct longing to never feel this horrible ever again.

She sat on the marble floor, her eyes closed and wondered if she had the strength to drive herself home. The task seemed impossible on a couple of different levels. First, she doubted she could make the trip without vomiting again. Second, she couldn't seem to focus on anything but how miserable she felt.

There was a knock on the bathroom door.

"Marina?"

She recognized Todd's voice. Why had this had to happen here of all places? With him around?

"Yeah?"

"How's your stomach?"

"Awful. I can't figure out what's wrong."

"I can. Food poisoning. All those cream sauces."

She remembered what they'd eaten and groaned. "You, too?"

"You bet. I got rid of Beatrice. Come on. I'll take you upstairs to one of the guest rooms. The bathrooms are more comfortable and you can crawl into a bed between events."

She hesitated for a second, then staggered to her feet. Stretching out on a bed sounded really good right now.

She opened the bathroom door and saw Todd looked about as bad as she felt. He was pale, slightly green and there were shadows under his eyes.

"Aren't we an attractive couple," she murmured as he took her hand and pulled her toward the stairs.

"We'll take a picture. We have to hurry. I don't know how long I have."

Despite how sick she felt, she started to laugh. "You sure know how to show a girl a good time."

"Tell me about it. At least it's Friday. You don't have classes on the weekend, do you?"

"No."

"Good. Then you can crash here as long as you'd like. There's a phone in your room if you need to call anyone. There are robes in the closet. I put a couple of my T-shirts on the bed, so you could sleep in something more comfortable than your clothes."

They reached the second-floor landing. She glanced at him. He'd thought of all that while feeling as horrible as she did? Talk about a great guy. "Thanks. You're going way beyond what's expected."

He put a hand to his stomach. "It's going to be an ugly few hours. Basically we have to get all the bad food out of our system."

She didn't want to think about that. "We should—"

Todd cut her off with a shake of his head. "Third door on your right. T-shirts on the bed. Water on the nightstand."

He turned and hurried in the opposite direction, ducking into a door at the far end of the hall.

Marina watched him go, then felt a faint rising in her own midsection. She didn't have much time herself.

She ran into the guest room and found everything as he'd described. There were two clean T-shirts on the bed, three bottles of water on the nightstand and a robe in the closet. But before she could deal with any of that, she ran toward the bathroom and wondered if she could possibly survive the day.

Six

Marina woke up sometime around six Saturday morning. She'd spent quality time in the bathroom until about midnight, then had crawled into bed and slept like the dead. After brushing her teeth with a conveniently placed new toothbrush, she slipped into the fluffy robe and headed out into the vast expanse of Todd's house to find the kitchen.

Passing through the dining room, still littered with flowers, she made her way toward the rear of the house and walked into a kitchen that could easily satisfy the pickiest chef known to man.

She also found Todd there. He wore sweats, a T-shirt and hadn't shaved. There was a slight shifting in her stomach, but this one had nothing to do with the food she'd eaten and everything to do with how delicious the man in front of her looked.

"Morning," she said, doing her best to act normal around the sudden fluttering in her chest. What was wrong with her? This was Todd. A guy she borderline despised. Except she couldn't. Not really. He'd been just as sick as she had been yesterday, but he'd taken the time to get her settled before spending his evening in his own bathroom.

He looked up and smiled. "Hey. How you feeling?"

"Better. My stomach is so empty I can practically hear coyotes howling. You?"

"I wrapped things up about one in the morning, then crashed. I'm going to make an executive decision here and say no to the cream sauce caterer."

She laughed. "I won't fight you on that. I don't think I've ever been that sick."

He nodded at the kettle on the stove. "At the risk of sounding like a wuss, how about some tea and dry toast? I think that's about all I can handle this morning."

"Sounds great. We probably need to hydrate."

He grinned. "That was a lot of fluids coming out."

"Tell me about it." She fingered the robe. "This is nice. Am I the first English speaking female to wear it?"

He leaned against the counter and crossed his arms over his chest. "You were going to let the model thing go."

"I don't remember saying that."

"You should." He looked her up and down. "It's for company, not dates. I don't usually bring women here, remember?"

"But your car is a little small for the wild thing."

He raised an eyebrow. "You're mighty curious about my personal life."

"Men love to talk about themselves."

"We usually go to her place."

"I see. That makes it easier to escape when you feel the need and doesn't push the money thing into their face."

"Exactly."

The kettle began to whistle. At the same time, bread popped out of the toaster.

"Dishes?" she asked.

He pointed to a row of cabinets. It only took her two tries to find small plates. She put the toast on a plate and popped in two more slices, while Todd poured water into a teapot. She glanced over his shoulder and saw fresh tea leaves in a little basket.

"Very fancy," she said. "Yours?"

"Apparently. I e-mailed my housekeeper last night and asked her if I had any tea. She said I did and told me where to find everything."

Imagine having so much stuff, you didn't know what you owned or where it was. Different worlds, Marina thought. Very different worlds.

They sat at the round table by the large window. She nibbled on a piece of toast, then took the mug of tea he offered.

"Interesting house," she said after she'd sipped the steaming liquid. "Kind of intimidating."

"It does leave an impression."

She looked at his face, at the dark stubble shadowing his cheeks and jaw. "How do you know it's ever about you?" she asked. "Nothing about your life is normal. How can you be sure?"

"I'm not. Even you agreed to go out with me after your grandmother offered you a million dollars."

She rolled her eyes. "Oh, please. You know that's just a joke. Although it is fascinating that she does think she has to pay someone to marry you. What does she know that I don't?"

"I'm ignoring the question," he told her.

Marina took another bite of toast and chewed slowly. So far her stomach was staying pretty settled, but she wasn't ready to get wild for a few more hours.

"You have to have been sure sometime," she said. "There have to be some women you trust."

"You don't want to talk about this."

"Are you asking me or telling me?"

His dark gaze settled on her face. "I went to an all-guys boarding school for high school. Ryan and I both did. My first serious girlfriend was a scholarship student at the all-girl school next door. We met at a dance and I fell for her in seconds. She was smart, funny and totally into me."

Marina didn't doubt that for a minute. She had a feeling he'd been the kind of guy a lot of girls would have been totally into.

"Her mother was barely making it, working in an office somewhere. Jenny told her about me. We were each other's first time." His face tightened. "Jenny's mom went to my parents and said that either they would pay her two hundred and fifty thousand dollars or she would bring me up on rape charges. Jenny was only sixteen, so there was a chance the charges would stick."

Marina felt sick again, although this time it had nothing to do with food poisoning. "I can't believe that. How horrible. How old were you?"

"Sixteen. But that didn't matter. My parents paid her off and I learned an important lesson."

She wanted to tell him that he'd learned the wrong thing, that people weren't like that, except she thought for him, maybe they were.

"What did Jenny have to say?" she asked.

"She was upset, or so she said. The week after we broke up, her mother bought her a car. That seemed to help."

He sounded bored and cynical, but talking about the past had to be hurting him. That sort of experience would leave a scar.

"Another woman I was dating came to me and said she was pregnant. I was always careful, but I had no reason to think she was lying. I did the right thing and asked her to marry me. She'd always talked about a big wedding, so I suggested we wait until after the baby was born, so the plans weren't rushed. She freaked at that."

Marina slumped back in her seat and closed her eyes. "Let me guess. She wasn't really pregnant?"

"No. She had a friend who peed on the stick and that's what she showed me. Apparently her plan was to try to get pregnant right away and if that didn't work, to 'lose' the baby right before the wedding. We would both be so devastated by the tragedy that we'd get married anyway."

"I hate that there are people like her in the world," she said. "I know the money makes it difficult, but you have to have had some good experiences with women."

"Some. A few. But I'm never sure. One way or another, I'm waiting for each one to finally admit it's all about the money."

She leaned toward him. "Todd, you're a great guy. You're smart and funny and charming and not half-bad looking."

He smiled. "Wait. I need a moment to bask in the 'not half-bad looking' compliment."

She laughed. "You know what I mean. It's not always about the money. It can't be. There aren't that many horrible people in the world."

"Before Ryan fell for your sister, he was dating a single mom with an adorable little girl. Ryan was convinced he'd found the perfect woman. He was crazy about the kid, wanted them both in his life and proposed. Then I overheard her talking to a friend about how she'd hated having a baby until she realized that most young, rich guys are suckers for a cute little girl. That she planned to stay married to Ryan for a couple of years, then divorce him and live on the child support he would offer to pay."

Her heart ached for Todd. "So what do you do? Never trust? Never care too much? Never put yourself out there?"

"It's working so far."

"But that's so lonely. Don't you want to be in love?"

"Not bad enough to get taken. I can get a woman whenever I want. If I need another heartbeat in the house, I'll get a dog."

Sadness nearly overwhelmed her. On the surface, Todd had everything, but in truth, there were big holes in his life. He was powerful and in charge—the sort of man who thrived on doing. He was also surprisingly kind and caring. And he would never trust a woman enough to truly give his heart.

"What are you thinking?" he asked.

"That we're both seriously twisted. You can't trust anyone else and I can't trust myself."

"I don't believe that," he told her. "You have it all together. Don't you date nerdy guys who are going to change the world?"

"Most of the time. They're brilliant and interesting and…" She bit her lower lip. They were supposed to be talking about him, not her.

"And safe?" he asked, his voice low.

"Maybe. Sometimes. I just…" She took a sip of the tea. "My mom fell in love with my dad the second she saw him. She was seventeen and to this day, she still adores him. My dad isn't a bad person, but he's not the greatest husband and father. He leaves. He just up and disappears for months at a time. We never know when he's going or how long he'll be gone. Every time he walks out, her heart breaks. But she won't tell him he can't come back. She won't let herself love anyone else. She lives a half-life, only truly happy when he's with her."

"You're not like that," he told her. "You're tough."

"You don't know that and neither do I. I'm terrified I'm just like her. That I'll fall for a guy who'll break my heart and I'll let him. I'll say it's okay. Falling in love, really falling in love, seems too much like handing over control of my life. It's not on my to-do list anytime soon."

"So instead of taking a chance, you date guys you're not at risk of falling in love with."

She looked at him. "Do you really want to spend much time pointing out my flaws, because I think you're in kind of dangerous territory."

"I'm willing to risk it. Am I right?"

"Maybe."

"You're always the object of affection, never the one at emotional risk."

"You're making me sound mean and I'm not. I just don't want to fall for anybody until I'm sure I won't be destroyed."

"You can never be sure."

"I refuse to believe that," she said. "One day I'll take a chance."

"Will you?"

She wanted to believe she would. That one man would be worth her step of faith.

"Obviously we both need therapy," she said. "Maybe we could get a group rate."

He laughed. The sound made her feel good inside. Then she yawned.

"Sorry," she said as she covered her mouth. "I didn't get enough sleep last night."

"Me, either." He rose. "Come on. Let's go to bed."

She stared at him. A thousand thoughts raced through her mind. Bed? With him? As in sex? She wanted to be shocked and insulted. She wanted to stand up and slap him. But as images of them together, naked, touching, filled her brain, she found herself just as interested in saying yes.

Todd held up both hands. "Sorry. Poor word choice. Let me start over. Let's go upstairs where we can each sleep in our own beds. Better?"

She nodded, because that was what he expected, but inside, she felt a sharp stab of disappointment. What was up with that?

He waited until she'd risen, then put a hand on the small of her back and guided her out of the kitchen.

"We'll meet up later," he said cheerfully, "and figure out if we ever want food again."

"Sounds like a plan."

At the top of the stairs, they each went their separate way. But as she closed the door of the guest room she couldn't help thinking how much she was wishing he'd meant what he said the first time.

Later that afternoon, Marina stepped out of the shower and reached for a towel. Todd might not invite a lot of lady friends to his place, but he kept the guest room well stocked. In addition to the toothbrush and toothpaste she'd found earlier, there was also shampoo, conditioner, body wash and an assortment of moisturizers.

After slathering on a yummy citrus-scented lotion, she dressed, gave her hair a halfhearted blow-dry and headed downstairs.

She was starving and tea and toast wasn't going to cut it. She figured she could do drive-through on her way home. But first she had to find her host and thank him for everything.

The kitchen was empty, as was the family room. She heard a faint noise, like someone typing on a keyboard and headed in that direction. She located Todd in a panel-lined study that looked like a set out of *Masterpiece Theater.* He was dressed, as well, and looked just as good as he had that morning.

Little tingles broke out all through her body. She felt a distinct flicker of heat and several other unwelcome physical responses.

"How are you feeling?" he asked when she walked into the room.

"Good. I slept more and now I'm starving."

"Me, too. So we both survived our food poisoning."

"Looks that way."

He stood and walked around the desk. "You ready to head home?"

She nodded, even though what she actually wanted to do was throw herself into his arms and beg him to take her. Obviously she was still suffering the ill effects of the bad food.

"Big date tonight?" he asked.

"Not really."

He picked up a folded piece of paper from his desk and offered it to her. "Because I remember you saying you loved Mexican food and there's a great place nearby that delivers. Want to have something to eat before you go?"

She hesitated. Her head told her to get out while she

was emotionally in one piece. The rest of her body—especially the exquisitely female bits—suggested she stick around and see how this might play out.

"We could watch a movie," he said. "I'll even let you pick."

She grinned. "How can I resist that kind of an invitation? What are the odds we'll agree on any movie?"

"There has to be at least one. Something funny."

"But smart, not silly."

"I have that."

"I never thought I'd eat again," Marina admitted three hours later as she stretched out on Todd's sectional sofa in his media room. "But I'm kinda hungry."

Todd sat slumped down with his stocking feet propped up on the suede covered ottoman in front of the sofa.

The fabric on the furniture and the carpeting were the only things soft about this high-tech space. There was a screen that looked as if it belonged in a movie theater, enough speakers to levitate a house, players and recorders and a collection of movies that had made her mouth water. It was man toy heaven.

"A taco, two enchiladas, chips, salsa and a salad weren't enough for you?" he asked as he glanced at her.

She grinned. "Apparently not. I'm kind of in the mood for dessert."

"Then let's go see what's in the kitchen."

He stood and stretched. They were both casually dressed—her in the clothes she'd worn the previous day, him in jeans and a loose T-shirt. As he raised his arms above his head, the hem of his T-shirt crept above the waistband of his jeans, exposing a sliver of skin and his belly button.

It shouldn't have been the least bit erotic. They'd spent the whole night throwing up and doing other disgusting things only a few dozen yards apart from each other. Yet as she watched him, she felt more than a little bit of wanting deep inside.

"You ate a bunch, too," she said as he led the way out of the media room and toward the staircase. "More than me."

"Feeling defensive about your very unladylike appetite?"

"Maybe. I was hungry."

"I won't tell anyone."

She elbowed him in the side. "It's not like I ate with my hands or anything."

He looked at her and raised his eyebrows. "You had tacos. Of course you ate with your hands."

"You know what I mean."

At the bottom of the stairs, she forgot where the kitchen was and went right. He went left and they slammed into each other.

"Sorry," she said as she took a step back.

He grabbed her upper arms and held her steady. "You feeling all right?"

"I'm fine. Just a lousy sense of direction."

His eyes stared into hers. She suddenly felt both vulnerable and incredibly alive. She wanted him to move those hands, to touch her everywhere. Even as her brain screamed out that this was potentially dangerous, she found herself taking a step closer.

She saw the exact moment he felt it, too. There was a sharpening of his features, a subtle tension in his body. Hunger darkened his eyes.

He dropped his hands and stepped back. "Dessert," he said. "We were going to get you some dessert."

"Right. Anything but ice cream."

He groaned. "We're scarred for life."

"I don't think so. I will bravely overcome my fear of cream anything to indulge in chocolate chocolate chip again. It's just the kind of person I am."

He led the way to the kitchen. So neither of them was willing to act on the attraction. Smart, she thought, even as she wrestled with disappointment. Still, there were complications. They were practically related and it wasn't as if he would disappear from her life once the wedding was over. Did she really want to spend the next fifty years sitting at the same table as Todd and have a single night of passion between them? Talk about awkward.

So she ignored the way he moved as he opened the freezer and pulled out an assortment of goodies. There were individual slices of cake, a pie that only needed to be defrosted, then heated, and brownies. In the pantry they found boxes of cookies and some chocolate chips that could work in a pinch.

"What will it be?" he asked.

"Brownies. I'll be putting frosting on mine. I noticed a can in the pantry."

"Because there's not enough sugar in a regular brownie?"

"Exactly."

"Women," he muttered as he pulled the tray of brownies out of the freezer. "We're going to have to microwave these to defrost them."

"I'm an expert at that sort of thing."

She reached for the brownies as he handed them over. But their timing was off and the plastic-wrapped tray slipped through her fingers to crash onto the floor. They both bent over at the same time and bumped heads. Marina slipped and landed on her butt.

"We're a hazard together," she said as she started to laugh. "A complete disaster. I thought both of us getting food poisoning was the worst of it, but apparently not."

He laughed, then sank down next to her on the floor. "You're not like other women."

"I could work on a charming European accent if you want."

He narrowed his gaze. "Let it go."

"Never."

He reached over and tucked a strand of hair behind her ear. "I never thought getting as sick as we did would be fun, but this has been. You don't need to rush home tonight if you don't want to. You could stay."

She knew how he meant the invitation. She could stay in the guest room. It was a polite and well-meaning invitation.

"A sleepover," she teased.

She looked at him, expecting to see an answering

smile. Instead she found heat, desire and a need that made her weak. Then he blinked and it was gone.

Her insides clenched, her heart began to beat faster and her throat when dry. "Todd?"

"I'm trying to be smart here, Marina. I can come up with a hundred reasons why this isn't a good idea."

She pressed her lips together. "A hundred. Wow. I can only come up with about eight."

"I might have been exaggerating." He stood and held out his hand. "Come on. We'll defrost brownies and lose ourselves in the sugar."

"Sounds like a plan."

She put her fingers against his palm and allowed him to pull her to her feet. When she was standing, she found they were really close together. She would have stepped back, but he didn't let go of her.

She let herself get lost in the fire in his eyes. It warmed her and enticed her, and she swayed toward him.

"Damn," he muttered, right before he reached for her.

Seven

His mouth was warm and smooth and when he kissed her, Marina felt heat clear down to her feet. Her toes curled, her thighs trembled, her midsection tightened and her breasts pouted because they wanted some attention, too.

He pulled her close and she let him because she needed to be pressed against the hard planes of his body. She wrapped her arms around his neck and leaned in, making sure they touched everywhere.

He explored her mouth, kissing lightly, gently, but with enough passion to keep her breath locked in her throat. There was a promise in his kisses, a promise that there would be a whole lot more in the near future. As the anticipation was nearly as amazing as what he was already doing, she was willing to wait.

As he continued to tease, rubbing his lips against hers, nibbling, pressing, but not quite taking, she explored the hard muscles of his shoulders and upper back. She ran her fingers through his hair, then raked her nails lightly across his nape.

Wanting poured through her, pooling low in her belly, and her most feminine center ached to be taken.

Finally he tilted his head and touched her lower lip with the tip of his tongue. She parted instantly, welcoming him inside. At the first intimate stroke, a shudder raced through her. Passion grew until her skin felt too tight, too sensitive, too impossibly needy.

She clung to him through deep kisses that touched her soul, through his hands moving up and down her back, until he cupped her rear and she instinctively arched toward him only to encounter the impressive hardness of his desire.

She gasped as she imagined him filling her over and over again. She wanted with a desperation that made her rub herself against him, like a lonely cat. Hunger made her frantic. She'd been very comfortable not dating, not getting involved, not having a man in her life. Suddenly she was starving for contact, for skin on skin nakedness. But not just with anyone…only Todd could scratch this particular itch.

Some of her need must have gotten through to him. Or maybe it was the quick pace of her breathing and the way she clamped her lips around his tongue and sucked. Whatever the method of communication, he seemed to get the message. He moved his hands to her hips, eased them under her long-sleeved T-shirt and rode her curves up to her breasts.

He caressed her with the skill of a man who loves women. Even through the fabric of her bra, she felt the gently but purposefully caress of his fingers. He cupped her, then used his thumbs and forefingers to tease her nipples into a frenzy.

Fire shot through her, diving down between her legs and stirring everything up. She couldn't think, couldn't breathe, could only stand there lost in the pleasure of him touching her. Her only conscious thought was to wonder how much better it would be if she wasn't wearing a bra.

Todd took advantage of her inattention to kiss his way along her jaw, then down her neck. He nipped her earlobe, kissed the sensitive area just below, then traced wildly erotic patterns with his tongue.

The combination of sensations was pretty incredible. She felt herself tensing in anticipation of release that couldn't possibly happen. Not like this. Sure it had been a long time, but she had some pride, didn't she? Shouldn't she at least let him take her jeans off before she gave in to passion?

But as he continued to tease and touch and play with her breasts, she found herself getting closer and closer. Apparently he realized it, as well, because he leaned in and murmured, "We need to get you into bed."

Before she could say anything, he'd grabbed her hand and tugged her out of the kitchen and into the hallway. She hurried alongside of him, eager to get upstairs, get naked and fall into paradise.

They started up the stairs.

"Is sex better on five hundred thread count sheets?" she asked.

He stopped, laughed, then pulled her close. "Of course," he said, right before he pulled her T-shirt over her head and kissed her.

She went willingly into his embrace, kissing him back, needing him more than she'd ever needed anyone.

Even as his tongue stroked hers, she felt him reach for the hooks on the back of her bra. Seconds later, the scrap of lingerie drifted down her arms and onto the stairs.

He broke the kiss and bent his head to take one of her breasts into his mouth. There was immediate heat as he sucked deeply, then circled her nipple with his tongue.

She swayed slightly, then put her hands on his shoulders to steady herself. The powerful pull of his mouth caused every nerve ending to quiver in delight. Between her legs there was dampness and heat and anticipation. More, she thought hazily. She needed more.

But for now, this would be enough.

He used his fingers to mimic the movement of his tongue, caressing both her breasts, forcing her into a higher and higher state of arousal until she knew it would take almost nothing to push her over the edge.

"Todd," she breathed, wanting her release, yet wanting to hang on for a little bit longer.

"Tell me about it," he muttered, then grabbed her hand and pulled her up the last few stairs.

They hurried down the hall and burst into a bedroom the size of lecture hall. She had a brief impression of warm colors, massive dark furniture and a big, comfy, inviting bed.

Finally, she thought as he released her hand and yanked off his T-shirt.

They were barefoot, so it didn't take much manipulation on his part to get them both naked. One second she was topless, then next her jeans and panties were pooling on the floor. His jeans and briefs followed. Then he was easing her back on the mattress and she was in his arms and they were touching skin on skin and it was glorious.

He stared at her, his dark eyes bright with passion. She traced his mouth, then smiled when he gently bit down on her finger.

"I want you," he told her. "You're sexy as hell."

"I find you mildly interesting, as well," she said.

He grinned. "Mildly, huh. So I have some work to do."

"Absolutely." Brave words from a woman on the edge, she thought happily.

"I don't mind getting down and dirty now and then." He shifted so he was next to her, on his side, his hand supporting his head. "Where should I start? Here?" He put his hand on her belly.

While that felt nice and all, it wasn't exactly what she wanted. "Um, no."

"Here?" He ran his fingers from her wrist to her elbow.

She shifted slightly. "Not what I had in mind."

He slipped his fingers between her legs and rubbed her swollen flesh. "How's that?" he asked, his voice low and husky.

It took every ounce of self-control to keep her eyes

open. She desperately wanted to fall into a passionate trance and get lost in her orgasm, but not just yet.

"That works," she breathed as he explored all of her, finding her center and rubbing it.

Tension rose up inside of her. Muscles tensed. She let her legs fall open in a blatant and time-honored tradition of invitation.

"Good. What about this?"

He leaned toward her and stroked her nipple with the tip of his tongue.

It was an amazingly perfect combination. It was exquisite, it was magic, it was more than enough to make her lose control.

She did her best to hang on, to at least take three minutes to come. But he began to move his fingers faster and faster, with the perfect amount of pressure. Then he sucked on her breast.

It was incredible. She pulled her knees up and dug her heels into the bed. Not yet, she told herself. Not yet. Not…

It was too late.

She fell into her release, caught in the waves of sensual pleasure that swept through her. Every part of her sighed in relief as he continued to touch her, easing her onward until her muscles gave out in sheer exhaustion.

Lethargy stole through her. She had to force herself to open her eyes and when she did, she found Todd staring at her.

She'd expected a self-satisfied male smile—one that more than hinted at his expertise and how everything had felt so good because he was so darned talented in bed. Instead he looked serious and intense and instead of smiling, he leaned in and kissed her.

She parted her lips for him and felt the lethargy fade. As his tongue teased hers, passion returned and she found herself eager to have him inside of her.

He was hard…she could feel him pressing into her leg. She reached between their bodies and lightly stroked his arousal. But instead of reaching for a condom and then entering her, he slid down her body, kissing first her neck, then between her breasts, along the center of her rib cage, her belly, before coming to rest at the top of her right thigh. He parted her swollen flesh with his fingers.

While she appreciated the gesture, it wasn't required. "I've already…"

Then he did smile. "I know. I was there."

Her mouth curved in response. "It was great."

"I'm glad. Now let's do it this way."

A man on a mission, she thought as she let her eyes slowly close. Far be it from her to tell him his attentions weren't welcome.

Her stomach clenched in anticipation of his touch. She felt a faint breath of air, then a warm tongue began to explore her.

She groaned as he circled around her still-swollen center. A quick, light brush and then he was gone, caressing the rest of her, getting close, but not actually touching her *there*. It was exquisite torture. It was incredible.

She parted her legs even more and drew back her knees. Heat burned through her as he kissed and licked and sucked everywhere but that one place she wanted the most.

There it was again. One brief moment of exquisite contact, then nothing. One hint of what she could be feeling, then only anticipation.

She began to squirm. She got closer and closer, but knew she couldn't find her release until he focused on that one place. Until he finally—

His tongue brushed her again. She nearly screamed from the glory of the contact, then prepared herself for him to move away. She was an adult and she wouldn't whimper. Only this time he didn't stop. He stayed in that one spot, licking and circling, teasing, arousing, pushing her closer and closer until her climax became as inevitable as the sunrise.

He intensified his attention and she was lost.

The shuddering began deep inside of her midsection and worked its way out. Her thighs trembled, her hands shook and then she was launched into a release so powerful, she truly thought she might never experience anything like it again.

He continued to kiss her, teasing her into coming and coming. She gave herself over to him, letting him take all of her, until the tension finally eased and she was still.

Todd sat up and looked at Marina. A flush stole across her chest and climbed to her cheeks. She was limp, but if the smile was anything to go by, also incredibly satisfied.

Her golden-blond hair spilled across his pillow in sexy disarray and when she opened her eyes, her pupils were so dilated, he could barely see any of the blue.

"Wow," she said, her voice thick and husky. "I don't even know what to say."

He'd been complimented before. Most women made it a point to gush and while he appreciated the praise, he'd sometimes wondered how much of it was earned and how much of it had to do with his bank account.

Marina wasn't like that. Somewhere in the process of planning the wedding, they'd become friends. He liked her. He thought she was funny and smart and sincere. How often could he say that about the women in his bed?

Which made this experience different. He couldn't remember the last time he'd made love with a friend.

She put her hand on his arm and urged him closer. "So far this had been a pretty one-sided show."

At her words, he once again became aware of the pressure of his arousal.

He opened the nightstand drawer and pulled out a condom. After slipping it on, he knelt between her thighs. She reached for him and guided him inside.

Immediately he got lost in the sensation of tight, wet heat. She surrounded him, drawing him in, letting him fill her.

Her scent teased him. He could hear her breathing, feel the light stroking of her hands on his back and sides. For once he wasn't thinking about how quickly he was going to have to get away once this was over. For once he could just enjoy the experience and let the rest of it go.

He pumped harder, faster, in and out, losing himself in the growing pressure. She wrapped her legs around his hips, urging him closer. Her body tightened around him and he was lost.

* * *

"This is not a good idea," Marina murmured, even as she held out her wineglass. "Twenty-four hours ago, I was curled up like a dog on the bathroom floor. I should give my stomach time to recover."

"It has," Todd said confidently. "Besides, you were the one who was going to put frosting on perfectly good brownies. Isn't this better?"

The "this" in question was a bottle of red wine. It was after midnight. She and Todd had made love a second time then dozed off, only to wake up starving. He'd pulled on jeans and had given her a T-shirt to wear, then they'd made their way to the kitchen where they'd found mostly defrosted brownies on the counter.

She inhaled the scent of the wine, then took a sip. It was smooth and dark, with absolutely no bite. "Not bad. Let me guess. You have a wine cellar in the basement."

"The house doesn't have a basement, but there is a temperature and humidity controlled wine cellar."

"Naturally." She thought of the lone bottle of chardonnay she kept in her refrigerator...for special occasions, of course. "And if I wanted a bottle of Dom Pérignon?"

He shrugged. "What do you think?"

That he wasn't what she'd expected. That he was a whole lot better and that made him dangerous.

She took the brownie he offered, then followed him to the sofa in the family room. At some point he must have turned on a stereo because she could hear soft music in the background.

They sat facing each other, the night settling in

around them. She felt a sense of intimacy and connection—neither were very smart.

"Todd," she began, not sure exactly what she wanted to say.

"I know."

"How can you? *I* don't even know what I was going to say."

He set his wineglass and brownie on the coffee table, then leaned in and kissed her. "You're going to say that this is a complication neither of us needs. That we have a wedding to plan and that we're about to become related by marriage—again. That staying friends instead of lovers makes the most sense."

"Okay, yeah, that's probably what I was going to say," she admitted, letting herself get lost in his dark eyes. "Not that tonight wasn't great."

"Agreed."

"And that you're not nearly as toady as I thought you'd be."

He raised an eyebrow. "Toady?"

She grinned. "You know what I mean."

"You mean I'm sophisticated and charming. A man of the world, unlike the boy-nerds you usually date."

"Something like that. And I'm refreshingly intelligent and together, with just a hint of sass and a fabulous grasp of the English language, unlike those stick figures you usually date."

"You are all those things," he said and kissed her again. Then he wrapped his arms around her and eased her onto her back on the sofa.

She stared up at him. "We'd agreed this was a bad idea to continue."

"We'll end things tomorrow," he said as he kissed his way along her jaw.

"It is tomorrow."

"Not until the sun comes up. That means we have all night."

She wrapped her arms around him and gave herself up to his seduction. All night sounded just about perfect to her.

"They're arguing about the color of the shutters," Willow said as she carefully pulled an impossibly tiny plant from the soil and carefully placed it in a plastic container. "I'm sorry I ever mentioned shutters. I don't mind handling the remodel, but I hate it when they start e-mailing me separately."

Marina found herself mesmerized by the quick and expert movements of her sister's fingers. Willow poured in the potting mix, tapped it down, made a hole, plucked a slender plant from the tray and settled it in its new home.

"I'm thinking purple," Willow said. "You know—to match the elephants."

Marina blinked. "What elephants?"

Her sister sighed. "I knew you weren't listening to me. What's going on?"

"There are going to be elephants?"

"No." Willow sighed. "Marina, what's up? You're not yourself. Do you feel okay?"

If she ignored the faint protest of sore and stretched muscles, then she was exceptional. She and Todd had made love past dawn. While she was impressed with his ability to be ready time after time, she was also pretty pleased with her own performance. She would guess that she'd had more orgasms in the last twenty-four hours than maybe in all her previous life.

"I'm fine," she said. "Just a little tired."

"Uh-huh." Willow didn't look convinced. She walked to the door of the back room at the nursery and closed it, then put her hands on her hips and stared at her sister. "Start at the beginning and talk slowly. I don't want to miss anything."

"There's nothing to say." Which was a big, fat lie. "Well, not all that much."

"I'm going to stand here and glare at you until you tell me."

Marina smiled. "You're not actually glaring. It's more of a semiscowl."

"Marina!"

"Okay, okay. I'm fine. Everything is fine. It's just…" She felt her mouth curve up in a very satisfied smile. "Friday Todd and I did some tasting at a caterer. When I went back to his place to discuss flowers with a floral designer, I started to feel really bad. We both had food poisoning. I ended up spending the night there, practically chained to the toilet."

"And *that's* what you're smiling about?"

"No. But Todd was great. By yesterday we were feeling better. He asked me to stay—in the guest room. So we had dinner and watched a movie and then, well…"

Willow's eyes widened. "Ohmygod! You had sex with Todd Aston the Third. I'm going to get a million dollars!"

Marina held up both hands. "Number one, I'm not marrying him, so you can let your dreams of the million dollars go. If you're so hot to open a nursery, talk to Kane. He would do anything for you."

Willow shook her head. "No, thanks. I'm going to raise the money on my own. If you're not willing to marry to get it for me, then I'll get a loan or something. Which, by the way, is so not the point. You had sex with Todd?"

Marina smiled. "I did. It was great. He's nothing I'd imagined. I like him."

Willow moved close and hugged her. "That's great. Yea for you."

"It's not great. It's weird and uncomfortable and we're not going to be together that way again."

Willow stepped back and stared. "Excuse me? You're glowing. I've never seen you glow before. No one walks away from glowy sex."

"I will. We both will. We talked about it and this is the most sensible plan. Look, we're already related by marriage through Grandma Ruth. It's going to happen again when Julie and Ryan get married. Todd is in our lives forever. A relationship with him wouldn't go anywhere."

Willow returned to her plants. "Why not? He's single, you're single. That's an excellent start."

"We don't have anything in common. We're from different worlds. On a more basic level, he doesn't trust women at all. Having heard about his past, I kind of don't blame him. And I'm not totally healthy in that area, myself. I have issues."

Willow collected another plant. "You're not Mom. You're not going to lose yourself in a man."

"You don't know that."

"You don't, either. I know you're too scared to try. You've always chosen safe guys. Guys who adored you but who could never, in a million years, actually touch your heart. You've never risked falling in love, so you can't know what you'll do. None of us want to be like Mom. None of us want to give up everything for a man. So don't. Be strong. Be your own person. But take a chance."

It was really good advice. A sensible person might even consider it. But in this case, Marina refused to be sensible. There was too much to lose.

"Even if I let myself fall for him," she said. "He'd never love me back. He refuses to get that involved."

"There's always a first time."

"Not for him."

"You're wrong," Willow told her. "There's a first time for everyone. Look at Kane. But you have to be willing to take the chance. You can't find perfect happiness unless you're willing to risk the pain. Is a half life of being safe really worth never finding your soul mate?"

Marina thought about their mother. Naomi had only ever loved one man and she'd spent her entire life having her heart broken by him over and over again.

"The soul mate thing is highly overrated," she murmured.

"No, it's not," Willow insisted. "But love does require

faith. If you can't have that, you'll never know. What if Todd's the one? Are you really willing to let him walk away? At least Mom spends some of the time happy. When Dad's with her, all is right with the world. If she didn't have those moments of joy, the rest wouldn't be worth it."

Marina wasn't convinced those brief moments were worth anything. Not when the pain was so great and there was no escape. She'd lived her whole life without a soul mate and had done just fine. It would be a whole lot easier to get over what she'd never had than to risk being destroyed by a man determined to never give his heart.

Eight

Todd checked his watch. He'd arrived a couple of minutes early for his meeting with Marina at the bridal shop, but he wasn't worried about her keeping him waiting. She wasn't the type.

He'd wondered if seeing her again after their long night together would be awkward, but now that he was here, he only felt anticipation. Not a good thing, he thought grimly. She wasn't the type to play the no-strings game and he wasn't willing to accept anything else. Even for her.

So he would forget what happened and look at her only as his cousin's fiancée's sister. A distant acquaintance. Someone he liked, but didn't care about. Wasn't interested in. Wouldn't get involved with.

His good intentions lasted right up until she burst into the bridal shop, looking rushed and five kinds of gorgeous.

"I know, I know," she said as she stepped inside and grinned at him. "I'm a minute late. How you must resent me for treating you so badly. Next thing you know I'll be making you hold my purse while I try on clothes and call you snookums."

He laughed with her and their gazes locked. Within seconds the rest of the world ceased to matter. There was only this moment and the woman in front of him.

Wanting made him hard and need made him step toward her. The sensible part of his brain was outvoted. The only thing that made sense was Marina in his arms.

One of them moved first. He didn't know if it was him or her and it didn't matter. But before he could reach for her, a fortysomething saleswoman walked up to them and sighed.

"How wonderful," she said. "I can always tell when a couple is really in love. You two have brightened my day."

It was like being dropped headfirst in a big, icy pool of reality. He stepped back. Marina did the same and then they avoided looking at each other.

Great, he thought grimly. Now things were going to be awkward. He'd never wanted that. Making love with Marina had been the most fun he'd had in a hell of a long time. Not just the sex, although that had been record-setting. But just hanging out with her. Relaxing, being comfortable.

"We're, ah, not getting married," Marina said with a smile that looked more forced than happy. "I'm Marina

Nelson. You've spoken with my sister Julie. She's the bride who's hiding out in China right now and making everyone else do her dirty work for her."

"Oh, of course." The woman looked between them. "My mistake. I'm Christie."

Todd introduced himself and they all shook hands.

"I have some ideas of what your sister might like," Christie said. "She was very specific about all her no's, which makes things easier. I understand you'll be trying things on and then getting her feedback?"

Marina nodded.

"That's fine. Usually we don't allow brides to take pictures until they've actually put a deposit on the dress, but Julie made special arrangements with the owner, so we're good on that. You have a camera?"

Todd patted his suit jacket. "Right here."

"Good. All right, Marina. Let's dress you up like a bride. I understand you and your sister are about the same size and height?"

The two women disappeared down a hallway. Todd found a comfortable chair and a table full of financial and sports magazines. A few minutes later Christie appeared and asked if he would like anything to drink.

He accepted the offer of coffee, then settled in to read. But he couldn't seem to concentrate on the article. Instead he remembered Marina's teasing expression when she'd first walked into the shop and felt a return of the pleasure he'd felt at that moment.

What the hell was up with that? he wondered. Liking her wasn't one of his rules. Wanting more was even worse. He knew the danger inherent in the situation...the betrayal that would follow. It always had. No woman was to be trusted.

But for the first time in years he found himself wanting to break his own rules. To see if maybe, possibly, Marina was different, even though he knew she couldn't ever be.

Marina fingered the incredibly soft fabric of the wedding gown. Except for the basics, like cotton versus leather, she knew nothing about material. Only that whatever this one was, she wanted it in her life always!

Christie came into the dressing room and smiled. "You look beautiful."

Marina grinned. "I know you say that to all the brides, but right now, I don't care. I feel amazing. I love how this dress feels and moves."

Christie fastened the buttons Marina couldn't reach, then held open the dressing room door. "Come see how you look."

Marina had come in wearing jeans and a T-shirt, feeling frazzled, rushed and weird about seeing Todd again. But dressed in this flowing confection of a dress, she felt beautiful and girly and like a princess. Even the borrowed high heels, compliments of the salon, had fit.

She stepped in front of a three-way mirror and gasped. The dress was perfection.

The fitted, strapless bodice clung to her and made her look impressively chesty. At the waist, the dress cascaded down to the floor in layers and layers of fabric, each row shaped and draping like a flower petal, including the three or four foot train.

There was a hint of pearl in the fabric and it made her skin glow. The style would hide Julie's pregnancy, but was still elegant and to-die-for.

"Wow."

She glanced up and met Todd's gaze in the mirror. She smiled and spun in a slow circle.

"You like?" she asked.

She couldn't tell what he was thinking but she definitely liked the way he had to swallow before speaking.

"Incredible. Both the woman and the dress."

Man, did he have all the good lines, she thought, feeling herself react to his words and his presence.

Christie moved in and began tugging on the dress. "The style is flattering to many body types, although if your sister is built like you, then this should work perfectly. She needs one that's ready to go and this one is available. We'll clean it and get it altered right before the wedding. Can you move in it all right?"

Marina took a couple of steps. The dress swayed gracefully. "It's so fabulous."

"Good," Christie said. "Now let me put up the train and we'll see if you can dance in it."

Dance? Marina looked at Todd again. "Can you dance?"

"I'm practically a professional."

"Liar."

"Try me."

Christie looped the train, fastening buttons and hooks until there was an impressive bustle in the back. Then Todd stepped close and swept Marina into his arms.

She told herself none of this mattered, that it wasn't real. She was helping her sister, nothing more. Yet as they danced to an imaginary song, she felt something stir deep inside of herself. Something dangerous and wonderful and more than a little scary.

She made the mistake of looking into his eyes and found herself wanting to get lost there. His fingers tightened on hers. She shifted slightly closer. The layers of the beautiful dress kept her from feeling his body against hers, which was a serious drag.

"So lovely."

The comment came from an only slightly familiar voice. Marina looked up to see her grandma Ruth standing in the entrance to the bridal salon.

"Hello, my dears," the older woman said as she approached. "I know, I know, I'm not to meddle, but when Julie e-mailed that the two of you would be here this afternoon, I couldn't resist."

Todd released Marina and walked over to his aunt.

"Ruth," he said in obvious affection, then bent down and kissed her. "Watching Marina trying on wedding dresses isn't meddling."

"I'm sure Julie will be delighted to have one more opinion," Marina told her, then hugged and kissed her grandmother as she did her best not to feel or look guilty. She stepped back and turned in a slow circle. "What do you think?"

"That you're very beautiful and so is the dress." Ruth smiled at Todd. "Have you taken pictures?"

"Not yet. We were seeing if Julie could dance in the dress."

Was it Marina's imagination or had Ruth's eyebrows gone up just a little?

"An excellent idea," the older woman said. "I'm sure Julie appreciates your thoroughness."

Marina had the sudden thought that somehow her grandmother had guessed she and Todd had slept together. Heat burned on her cheeks as she tried to convince herself that wasn't possible. No one knew. Well, Willow and eventually Julie and maybe Ryan, but no one else.

Marina posed while Todd took several pictures, then she escaped back into the dressing room. She eased into a second gown, this one also strapless, but with a lace bodice and shirring across the waist. The skirt, a stunning, smooth silky material with an inset of embroidery and lace, fell in a sophisticated A-line that spilled into a train.

Ruth stepped into the dressing room. "Another winner. Julie's going to have a difficult time choosing. But that's the problem to have. Here, dear, let me help you with the buttons."

"Thanks. There are a lot of them."

Ruth stepped behind her and began fastening the cloth-covered buttons. "You and Todd looked very special together, dancing. While I always hoped one of you girls would fall for him, I'll admit I thought it was little more than the dreams of an old woman."

Panic welled up inside of Marina. "You're not old," she said by way of a very pitiful distraction.

"Thank you, dear, but that's not the point. I offered you and your sisters the money as a way to spur competition, but I see now I only needed to let nature take its course."

Marina's mouth opened, then closed. Her brain froze and she had no idea what to say.

"We're not a couple," she managed to say at last. "Seriously. We're barely friends. Semifriends, really. Acquaintances. We're helping with the wedding and that's all. We haven't even had our first date yet. That's not until the wedding."

Ruth finished with the buttons and stepped out in front of Marina. "Apparently a date isn't required. You look very beautiful."

Marina muttered something unintelligible, then hurried out of the dressing room as fast as she could on borrowed three-inch heels. Instead of stepping in front of the massive mirror, she hurried to Todd's side and grabbed his arm.

"She knows. My grandmother, your aunt, knows. She knows we had sex and I'm telling you right now, I can't stand it. I'm totally humiliated and you need to be, too."

Todd looked unconcerned. "She doesn't know. She can't."

"Want to bet?"

Ruth stepped out of the dressing room and Marina moved in front of the mirror. They discussed the dress like rational adults and she did her best to keep from blushing. She even managed a smile while Todd was taking pictures.

"I'll send these to Julie," he said.

"Great. I think she'll really love them."

Which all sounded normal, but what she was thinking was more along the lines of *get me out of here*.

Todd obviously didn't believe her, because he continued to joke with Ruth, right up until his aunt said, "I suppose a double wedding is out of the question."

Todd looked at Marina, then back at his aunt. "You mean Willow and Kane?"

"No, dear. You and Marina. There's obviously chemistry. Of course a relationship requires more than that, but passion is wonderful. I had it with your uncle every day of our marriage." She gave a little laugh. "Well, not *every* day, but most of them."

Marina resisted the need to cover her ears and hum loudly so she wouldn't hear anymore. Todd swallowed hard and muttered, "There's an image I'll never get out of my head."

Ruth sighed. "You young people. Never wanting to know about the older generation. You should be happy to know your uncle and I had a wonderful marriage all those years."

"I'm thrilled," Todd told her. "Details not required."

Ruth smiled. "That's all right. I've waited a long time for you to find the right girl and now you have."

Marina swept past him and headed for the dressing room. He followed on her heels.

"I told you," she said as she presented him with her back so he could unfasten the buttons. "But no. You wouldn't listen. You knew best. My *grandmother* knows we had sex. Do you know how humiliating that is?"

"It's worse for me. You never met my uncle, but I knew him all my life. Now I have a picture of the two of them…"

Marina spun to face him. "You're not taking this seriously enough. Ruth knows. She's talking about double weddings. She might tell my mother. I do not want to have a conversation about my sex life with my mother."

He touched her cheek. "Then don't. Look, telling Ruth wouldn't be my first choice, but she guessed. So what? We know what we want and don't want from each other. It's no big deal."

Apparently not for him, she thought bitterly, wondering if maybe he was right. If maybe she was overreacting.

Ruth stepped into the dressing room. "I have to leave, so you two enjoy yourselves. I hope it all works out. Truly I do. Not just because of what I want, but because all that money will really make a difference for your family, Marina. Sweet Willow can buy her nursery at last."

Then Ruth was gone, but Marina barely noticed. Instead her attention was riveted on Todd's face—on the way his features tightened and the distance she saw in his eyes.

He physically took a step back from her. "I'll leave you to get changed."

Then she was alone in the dressing room. Alone and angry and confused.

Why had Ruth had to mention the money like that? For a woman who was so set on getting them together, she'd picked the one way guaranteed to keep them apart. If Todd had a button, it was women wanting him for his money.

She wanted to stamp her foot in frustration. Talk

about unfair. She wasn't the least bit interested in his millions or billions or however much it was. The bet about marrying him was a joke. He had to know that.

Except why would he? Given his past, he would think the worst because the worst had always been true.

"It doesn't matter," she told herself as she stepped out of the dress. "We don't have a real relationship. We're just friends."

Friends who slept together.

But sex wasn't love and there was no way she was falling for him, so what did it matter that he thought badly of her?

Yet somehow it did matter and when she left the bridal salon a few minutes later, it was with a tightness in her chest and a sick feeling in her stomach.

To: Marina_Nelson@mynetwork.LA.com
From: Julie_Nelson@SGC.usa

Let me just say, for the record, that I'm stunned that you would sleep with Todd Aston the Third and not tell me. Even worse, I had to hear about it from my GRANDMOTHER! You slept with Todd? You slept with TODD? While I'm out of the country and we're so many time zones apart that I'll never hear the details?

I know you're telling Willow everything. I hate being left out. In time I'll forgive you, but know for now the sisterly bonds between us are stretched to the limit.

To: Julie_Nelson@SGC.usa
From: Marina_Nelson@mynetwork.LA.com

When did you become such a drama queen? The sisterly bonds? Someone's getting just a little too carried away by all this.

I'm sorry you had to find out from Grandma Ruth. I was going to tell you myself, but I didn't want to put that kind of information in e-mail. Obviously I'm the only one who worries about that sort of thing.

It was one time, or at least one night. It happened by accident. I'll explain the details later. They're actually kind of funny. But the point is, we're not a couple. We're friends who happened to sleep together and we have no plans for it to happen again.

To: Marina_Nelson@mynetwork.LA.com
From: Julie_Nelson@SGC.usa
That's it? That's all I get? How pathetic. I want details. And FYI…people don't accidentally sleep together. It's a conscious act/decision. You're not fooling me here, kid. So what's really going on?

Marina stared at the e-mail before answering. What *was* going on with her and Todd?

To: Julie_Nelson@SGC.usa
From: Marina_Nelson@mynetwork.LA.com
We're just friends. I swear. I like him, which I never thought would happen, but liking isn't anything more. Yes, we slept together, but there won't be a repeat performance and after this wedding is planned, we'll see each other at family events a few times a year and that's all. He's not the one. He's just a guy.

A special guy, she admitted to herself as she sent off the e-mail. But still, just a guy.

"I'm running late," Belinda yelled as Todd stepped into her photography studio. "Have a seat and I'll be with you in a bit."

He smiled at the receptionist, then made his way back to the large open space where she did most of her work.

Belinda, a petite redhead who dressed like a gypsy, stood in front of a camera and stared at the adorably dressed twins sitting on a bale of hay.

The identical little girls wore pink and white dresses and their dark hair had been carefully curled and styled.

"Okay—heads together," Belinda said with a grin, "but no bumping. Just touching at the top."

The girls complied.

"Now think about Christmas morning. What it's like to be awake but know it's too early to go downstairs. Remember how excited you feel. There are so many presents and soon you'll get to rip open that shiny paper and see what you got. It's so fun, but you have to wait. Think about that."

Both girls smiled, their eyes bright, their faces alive with anticipation.

Belinda snapped several pictures.

"She's good."

He turned and saw Marina had walked into the studio.

Their last meeting had turned awkward, thanks to Aunt Ruth. He waited for some feeling of discomfort, or a need to be anywhere but here. Instead anticipation swept through him and made him want to pull her close.

"The best," he said. "How are you?"

"Good. Busy with classes, but that's fun." She looked at the twins. "Adorable little girls."

"I agree."

"Really? You want kids?"

"Sure. A lot. I've always wanted my own baseball team."

She winced. "That's too many. But three or four would be a nice number. How do you plan to get these kids?"

He glanced at her. "I have no problem with having a family. It's having a wife I object to."

"So you'll adopt?"

Her eyes were the color of the sky. A perfect shade of blue. He liked how he could read her moods and how she wasn't intimidated by him. When this was over, maybe they could stay friends…assuming he got his burning need to make love with her again out of his system.

"Adoption is a possibility," he said. "But I would like a couple of biological kids to carry on the family name."

"Inherit the family money," she teased.

"That, too."

"So what will you do? Hire someone to carry the kids? Rent a womb, so to speak?"

He shrugged. "Maybe. It's an option."

Marina's eyes widened and her mouth dropped open. "I was kidding."

"I'm not. Everything is for sale."

"No offense, but that's really icky."

"Why? Surrogate mothers aren't uncommon. I'd have to be careful."

"Sure. What was I thinking?" She folded her arms over her chest. "It's a complicated choice. After all, the biological mother contributes fifty percent of the gene pool. Plus some scientific studies suggest intelligence is inherited through the mother."

"Which explains why a lot of successful guys who are more concerned about a beautiful woman than one with brains or character end up with disappointing children."

Disapproval radiated from her like fog. It surrounded him, trying to chill him, but he was unmoved. It was his life and he could damn well do what he wanted. If that meant kids without a wife, then that was his choice.

"You sound really cold-blooded," she told him.

"I'm being practical."

She drew in a breath, then released it. "Given your past, I understand your reluctance to trust anyone, but there's still a part of me that says you *can* have it all. You can fall in love, get married and have your kids the old-fashioned way. No contracts required."

"Is that what you want?" he asked.

"Sure. There's something wonderful about being a part of a family."

"You don't seem to be in a hurry to find Mr. Right."

Marina nodded. "I know I have my issues, but I'm willing to take a step of faith."

"Cheap talk."

"I'll get there. Eventually."

Would she? He doubted it. They might be very different, but they both had a fundamental lack of trust when it came to love. She was afraid of losing herself, the way her mother had, and he was determined to be more than a meal ticket.

"It takes faith," she told him. "One day I'll find someone who makes the leap worthwhile and then I'll jump."

Todd looked skeptical. "I hope he's there to catch you."

The photographer finished up with the children, then came over and hugged Todd, then introduced herself to Marina.

"I've never been hired from China before," the older woman said with an easy grin. "This could be fun."

"We'll e-mail Julie and Ryan some samples, if that's all right with you," Todd told her. "Marina and I will pick out a few."

"Sure. Great. I have my albums over here. I'll show you a big selection, then point out which ones are available to be sent digitally."

Marina watched the easy rapport between Belinda and Todd. "How did you two meet?" she asked.

Todd groaned, but Belinda laughed. Then she patted him on the cheek.

"Todd's parents hired me to take his picture for his sixteenth birthday. It was all very formal and solemn."

"So humiliating," Todd muttered.

Marina grinned. "That portrait wouldn't be in the sample albums, would it?"

Belinda shook her head. "He'd kill me if I put it

there, but maybe I can scan one of the proofs and send you a copy."

Marina leaned close to Todd and rested her head on his shoulder. "I would love that."

"You send it and I'll never forgive you," Todd told Belinda.

"Of course you will."

They spent the next half hour going over Belinda's samples. Her pictures were incredible. Romantic without being mushy, clear, artistic, yet timeless.

"She captures personalities," Marina said as she pointed at a wedding picture. "Look at the bride's smile. You can tell she's kind of wacky but fun."

"Yeah and he's crazy about her."

Looking at the happy couples made Marina feel a little empty. She wanted what they had—love and trust. Someone she could count on, no matter what. But this day wasn't about her.

"Any of these would be great," she said. "Let's just give Belinda Julie and Ryan's e-mail address and she can send whatever she wants. They're going to love her work."

They returned to her studio to tell her.

"Sure, I'll send a big selection," Belinda told them. "But before you go, let me snap a couple of pictures of you two. Having a familiar subject can be really helpful."

Todd looked at Marina who shrugged.

"I have a few minutes," she said, not exactly sure what Belinda was talking about.

"Good. I'm all set up for my next appointment. That will make this go quickly."

Belinda pointed at a muted backdrop done in blues and grays. There were lights all around and a camera in front of the backdrop.

"Stand in the middle," Belinda told him. "Close together. Let's try a traditional pose. Todd, put your arms around her waist. Marina, put your hands on top of his."

They did as they were told. Marina did her best to ignore the heat of Todd's body and the way his nearness made her thighs tremble. The longer he held her, the more she ached for him.

"Big smiles," Belinda said. "Come on, don't make me do the Christmas morning speech a second time today. It gets old. Think about something great. I know. The last time you had sex."

Involuntarily she glanced up at him only to find him looking down at her. She remembered everything about them being together that night. His touch, his laughter, the way he'd made her respond in ways she hadn't thought possible.

"Perfect," Belinda called. "Keep looking like that. Okay, now think of something funny—like Todd in a chicken costume, complete with a big chicken tail."

Marina felt her mouth twitch as she got the image in her mind. Then she started to laugh.

"Gee, thanks," he told her.

"You'd make a great chicken."

"My life is complete."

Marina was still laughing when Belinda told them they were done.

"I'll e-mail these pictures to Julie and Ryan, as well,"

she said. "I'm holding the date, so if you could let me know in the next week or so, that would be perfect."

"Will do," Todd promised.

"Thanks for everything," Marina told her. "You're amazing."

"Words I live to hear."

Marina followed Todd outside.

"We're still on for the wedding this Saturday, right?" he asked as they stopped by her car.

"You mean the wedding we're crashing? I'm braced."

"We're there to hear the orchestra. That's not crashing. We won't eat anything. It will be fine."

"I've never crashed a wedding before," she said. "That will make this very special."

"You'll like it."

She waved, then climbed into her car. He did the same and drove away first. But before she started her engine, she thought about what he'd said about having kids without a woman in his life. While she admired his desire to have a family, she was also sad at how he was limiting himself by refusing to trust anyone.

Ironically they were opposite sides of the same issue. He trusted himself, but no one else. She trusted everyone *but* herself. They both needed to take a leap of faith, but could they? And if they didn't, would they ever find their heart's desire?

Nine

Late Saturday afternoon Todd drove through Westwood toward UCLA. Marina had called earlier and asked him to pick her up on campus, instead of at her place, for their appointment to listen to the orchestra. She'd given him directions to one of the frat houses.

Now he found the correct street and turned right, then looked for the address. He spotted Marina before he saw the house. She stood on the lawn with a tall good-looking guy and they were gesturing at each other.

As he watched, the guy pulled Marina close and hugged her. She laughed and kissed his cheek.

Something dark and cold coiled low in his belly. He narrowed his gaze as Marina spoke using sign language. She obviously knew the other guy really well. But what the hell were they talking about?

They continued to gesture rapidly, then Marina turned, saw him and waved. The guy looked at him, hugged her again and turned back to the house.

As she walked toward his car, Todd was torn between being unreasonably pissed off and admiring the way her dress outlined her curves. He'd only ever seen her in casual clothes, so the high-heeled sandals, dangling earrings and upswept hair were a change.

"I'm ready for my night of crime," she said as she opened the passenger door and lowered herself onto the seat. "I thought about bringing masks so no one would recognize us, but then I was afraid we'd really stand out."

He ignored the humor and stared at the big house. "You date frat boys?"

"Date? Uh, no. That was David, one of the people I sign for. He's a senior, he has a hot date and his car died a couple of days ago, so I'm loaning him mine. Normally I wouldn't, but he's planning on proposing, so that seemed like a good cause to support."

He turned his attention to her and saw a combination of humor and exasperation in her eyes.

"I just wondered," he said defensively. "Frat guys have a reputation."

"Sure. That was the only reason for going all primitive on me."

"Primitive? Not my style."

Not ever. That would require jealousy and jealousy implied caring. While he liked Marina, theirs was a friendship.

"You're weird, Todd," she murmured. "You know that?"

"Not weird. Charming, handsome, sexy, mysterious."

She eyed him. "I'll give you complicated, but nothing else."

"You just don't want to admit how much you're attracted to me."

"As if."

But as she spoke, her gaze lingered on his mouth. He felt a rush of heat and need that had him shifting uncomfortably on the seat.

He pulled into traffic. "The reception is in Beverly Hills," he said. "We'll go in, smile politely, offer congratulations, listen to the music, then leave."

"Whatever you suggest," she told him. "You're the professional criminal. This will be my first time."

"We're just going to listen to music, that's not against the law."

"Criminals always have an excuse. Does Ryan know about your lawless ways? You guys are business partners—he should probably be protecting his assets. Next thing you know, you'll be pilfering."

He deliberately kept his expression stern. "I do not pilfer."

"Sure you don't. You're practically sainted. If your aunt Ruth could see you now."

Speaking of Aunt Ruth. "Did she call you?"

Marina looked at him. "My grandmother? No. Was she going to?"

So he'd been the only one. "No. Don't worry about it."

"You can't just bring up something like that and then drop it. What happened?"

"She's called me a couple of times since she dropped by the bridal place. There were a few unsubtle hints about us taking things to the next level."

Marina winced. "She wasn't talking about us sleeping together again, I'm guessing."

"Not exactly." Although his aunt had mentioned the whole "passion" issue several times, taking the conversation to a place Todd never wanted to go again.

"You're probably not going to think this is good news, but she also blabbed to Julie, who probably told Ryan."

He glanced at her. "Your grandmother told your sister we had sex?"

"Oh, yeah. I had a couple of very shouty e-mails from Julie. She's afraid she's missing out."

And he wanted a family why?

"What did you tell her?" he asked.

"That I'd share all the details when she got back." She smiled at him. "We're very close."

He had a feeling she was kidding. Or maybe that was wishful thinking on his part. Women did talk and he had no idea what they said to each other. Like every other normal guy on the planet, he didn't *want* to know.

"I'm sorry Ruth is being a pain," he said. "Can you ignore her or should I say something?"

"As I'm not the one she's calling, ignoring works for me. Are you going to have problems ignoring her?"

"No." He loved Ruth, but she didn't get to tell him

what to do. He knew she wanted him married and that wasn't happening.

"That sex thing was probably a mistake," Marina said quietly. "It's good we're never doing it again."

He thought about how great they'd been together. How much he'd enjoyed pleasing her, tasting her and touching her. How easily they'd talked and laughed. How much he still wanted her.

"I couldn't agree more," he said firmly.

The hotel was like something out of a movie, Marina thought as she and Todd strolled down wide, well decorated hallways to the ballroom overlooking the private garden.

They managed to slip inside without anyone asking them questions or accusing them of being there without an invitation, although she felt as if everyone in the room knew they were imposter guests.

"Relax," Todd said as he slipped an arm around her waist. "There have to be at least three hundred people here. No one will notice us."

"Okay, but no eating or drinking. We probably shouldn't even sit down and take a real guest's place."

He smiled a her. "You're not much of a rule-breaker, are you?"

"Only under very specific circumstances. Like the no more than four items in a dressing room rule. That one I'm good to break."

They circled the ballroom, avoiding the tables clustered at one end and staying toward the dance floor. A waiter came by and offered some kind of puff pastry treat. Todd reached for it, but she pushed his hand away.

"We're not supposed to eat," she told him, her voice low and insistent.

He chuckled. "You're making this too much fun."

"We're not here to have fun. This is serious. Okay, they're setting up to play. This is good. We can listen, then leave."

"Coward."

"I'm ignoring you." She watched the small orchestra seat themselves. "You're right—there aren't too many of them. So what are you thinking? The alcove in Grandma Ruth's ballroom?"

"Or that space between the pillars. The sound would be better coming from there."

"Good point. I just wish they'd start."

A well-dressed older couple moved toward them.

"Kitty and Jason Sampson," the woman said as she reached for Marina's hand. "How good of you to come."

Marina froze. They were caught!

But Todd smiled smoothly and responded. "Everything is lovely. Very impressive. Such a happy day."

Kitty beamed. "Isn't it? We're so delighted."

"Of course you are," Todd told her.

Jason leaned down and kissed Marina's cheek, then slapped Todd on the shoulder. "Thanks so much for joining us today. It means a lot."

"We wouldn't have missed this for anything."

The Sampsons left.

Marina waited until they were out of earshot, then

covered her face. "We're going to hell. I can hear them etching our names on our chairs."

"We get chairs in hell?"

She glared at him. "You know what I mean."

"Nothing happened. We were polite and gracious. In five minutes, Kitty and Jason won't remember us. Come on. You can handle this. Look, the orchestra is about to start."

"Maybe. It's not that I *want* to feel guilty," she began.

"Then don't. Come on. We'll lurk in the corner and stay out of trouble."

As he spoke, he grabbed her hand and pulled her to the side of the room. While his touch was totally casual, her body responded as if he'd just ripped off her dress and thrown her down on a table. Make that a bed…in a very private place, because her reaction was anything but outrage.

She melted from the inside out. The need to be with him nearly overwhelmed her, which was five kinds of crazy. They'd only been together that one night. Even though it had been a great time, it shouldn't have made that much of an impact on her.

Still, she found herself wanting to be with him, but not just in a sexual way. She wanted to be in his arms, talking and laughing. Watching him smile, listening to his voice and hearing his unique perspective on the world. She wanted…more.

"Better?" he asked as they stopped in a corner of the room, close to the orchestra but out of the flow of guest traffic. "We're practically acting like spies, hiding behind this potted tree." He fingered a leaf. "Do you know what this is?"

"Not a clue. That's Willow's area of expertise. It looks real, though." She allowed herself to relax. "Yes, this is much better. I can feel my guilt easing."

"Excellent."

He smiled at her. The answering quiver deep inside had something to do about his proximity, but not totally. Some of her reaction was just about him.

What was up with that?

Before she could figure out an answer, a waiter stopped by and offered them each a glass of champagne.

"The bride and groom will be here in a few minutes," he said. "This is for the toast."

Marina pulled free of Todd and tucked both her hands behind her back. "We can't," she whispered.

Todd took the two glasses and thanked the waiter. When the two of them were alone again, he offered one of the glasses.

"We have to," he told her. "Not toasting the bride and groom would be tacky and rude."

She bit her lower lip. "This is a very slippery slope. Okay, we'll raise our glasses, but we can't drink."

He grinned. "Right, because after we put the glasses down, someone else will gladly finish off the contents? Face it, kid. You're in this for a glass of champagne."

Marina sighed. "Maybe we can find out Kitty and Jason's favorite charity and make a donation."

"You're such a lightweight," he told her as he put his

arm around her waist and pulled her close. "I like that about you."

The quiver intensified.

A man who was probably the best man walked up to the microphone in front of the orchestra. "Ladies and gentlemen, will you please join me in welcoming Mr. and Mrs. Alex Sampson."

Everyone cheered as the bride and groom entered the room.

"A toast," the best man continued. "To a couple who defines love. May each day be better than the one before."

He raised his glass. The guests all did the same. Marina winced, then raised hers and took a tiny sip of the illicit champagne.

Todd leaned close. "Dom Pérignon."

"Really?" She took another sip. It was really nice. And honestly, if the families could afford that high-end champagne for the crowd, then maybe two stolen drinks weren't that big a deal.

"I'll accept the champagne," she murmured, "but we're not staying for dinner."

"Absolutely not. Just for one dance."

The orchestra began to play. The bride and groom stepped onto the dance floor and moved together.

Marina ignored them and instead focused on the smooth music. It was definitely more elegant than a DJ, but not really stuffy.

"Good choice," she told him. "I like the orchestra. Now let's go."

"Not so fast." He took her glass from her and set it

on a small table next to them. Then he led her toward the dance floor.

"What?" She tried digging in her heels, but it was a hardwood floor and that was not going to happen. "We can't dance."

"Why not? Everyone else is."

Sure enough several of the guests had moved into the center of the room and had joined the bride and groom. Marina decided that one dance wouldn't hurt. It wasn't as if they were eating anything. So she relaxed into Todd's arms and found out that he had yet another talent she'd never considered. This was even better than their spin around the bridal shop dressing rooms.

"You're good," she said after he'd twirled her around and then neatly caught her. "Lessons?"

"Years of them."

He pulled her close as the music slowed in tempo.

She rested her head on his shoulder. He had one of his hands on the small of her back. They pressed together in a way that was both sensual and enticing.

"We'll leave after this song," he said, speaking directly into her ear.

"Okay."

"You want to get something to eat?"

"Sure."

"Takeout?"

She raised her head and stared at him. Passion turned his eyes to the color of night.

He touched a finger to her mouth. "I know what

you're going to say," he told her softly. "That we agreed
we couldn't do this again. That it would be a mistake
for a lot of reasons. If that's what you want, I won't ask
again. I've spent the past week telling myself why I
have to let this go, but I can't. I want you, Marina."

They were words that would have cracked a wall a
whole lot tougher than hers. "You had me at 'takeout,'"
she whispered. "Let's go."

They went to his place because it was closer. The sev-
enteen-minute drive seem to last forever, possibly
because Todd spent much of the time nibbling on her
fingers. The combination of teeth and tongue and lips
was amazingly arousing. More than once she'd been
tempted to tell him to pull over and they could just do
it in the car.

She held back because it was daylight, she wasn't
into being an exhibitionist and because a night in jail
wasn't on her to-do list for that day. Of course Todd
hadn't been, either, but she did try to be flexible when
offered a wonderful opportunity.

They reached his house and piled out of the car. He
opened the front door, pulled her inside, slammed the
door shut behind her, flipped the lock and dragged her
into his arms.

She went willingly, already anticipating the heat of
his kiss.

He didn't disappoint. His mouth was firm and hungry
and he tasted like great champagne. Even as they
touched and strained and did everything they could to

climb inside each other, he swept his tongue into her mouth and began that passionate dance.

He circled her, teasing, exciting. She met him with moves of her own and then closed her lips around his tongue and sucked gently. He groaned. She felt his hardness press against her belly. She was already wet and swollen. Her breasts ached. Deep inside she clenched in anticipation of what was to come.

He pulled back slightly and nudged her backward. "Bed," he murmured against her neck. "Up. Go."

The instructions would have been funny if she hadn't been so eager. She forced herself to break free of his erotic kisses and hurried toward the stairs.

Before climbing, she kicked off her shoes. He did the same.

Halfway up, they stopped and kissed again. As he stirred her soul, he reached for her zipper and pulled. She pushed off his suit jacket, then began to loosen his tie. He pulled his shirt free.

While she wasn't usually overly aggressive in bed, Marina didn't think of herself as shy. So she took a step back, shrugged out of the dress and let it fall to her feet.

Underneath she wore a lavender lace bra and matching panties. Todd's breath caught audibly. She reached behind herself, unfastened her bra, let that fall, as well, then turned and ran up the stairs.

It took him a second to follow, but when he did, he caught up quickly. At the second-floor landing, he lunged for her, grabbing her and pulling her to a stop. She laughed and spun toward him.

He was standing a step lower. He tore off his tie, unfastened his shirt and tossed it down, then leaned in and took her right nipple into his mouth.

He sucked and licked and circled until she could barely keep standing. She had to hold on to his shoulders and even so, her legs shook. The deep tugs caused an answering response low in her belly.

When he moved to her other breast, she felt herself starting to lose her balance. He must have sensed it, too, because he put his arms around her waist and lowered her to the top of the carpeted stairs.

She went willingly, wrapping her arms around him and enjoying the feel of his hot skin.

He raised his head. "We *will* make it to bed," he told her.

"I'm in favor of that plan."

He smiled. "But first…"

He reached for her panties and pulled them off in one quick movement. Then he shifted down a couple of stairs, urged her to part her legs and kissed her between them.

The intimate caress took her breath away. She had to brace herself on her arms to keep from falling over and even that wasn't enough. Not with her already shaking in need.

He was as good as she remembered. Exploring, circling, stroking, licking, driving her to the edge, only to back off just enough to make her whimper.

Over and over he touched her with his tongue and his lips. He drew her higher and higher, pushing her forward, then letting her fall back. He made her pant. He nearly made her scream.

She lost track of the world and everything in it. There was only this moment and this man and what he was doing to her.

Her muscles clenched tighter and tighter. She could feel herself swelling, pushing close. Her orgasm was tantalizingly out of reach. Close, so close, but not yet there.

Then he began to flick his tongue over her center in an age-old rhythm. At the same time he inserted first one finger, then two. He filled her, pushing up as if to caress her from the inside, as well.

One stroke, two…and then she was lost.

Her release claimed her with an unexpected force. She lost control and cried out. She came again and again, riding the magic of his tongue, his fingers, his whole body. Pleasure claimed her, marked her, then eased her back into reality.

When she finally surfaced, he sat next to her, smiling.

She sat up and sighed. "Go ahead. Gloat. You earned it."

"I will in a second. Meet me in my bed, okay?" He stood.

"Where are you going?"

"It's a surprise."

He hurried down the stairs. She watched him go, still basking, then realized she was sitting naked on his stairs and she had no idea if this was housekeeper day or not. Which got her moving.

She found her way to his large bedroom and had

barely pulled back the covers when he walked into the room carrying two champagne flutes and a bottle of Dom Pérignon.

She laughed. "You did say you always had some on hand."

"I did."

While he opened the bottle, she climbed into bed. He poured them each a glass, took off the rest of his clothes and joined her.

"To unexpected surprises," he said, touching his flute to hers. "You more than qualify."

She opened her mouth, then closed it. She couldn't speak, couldn't move, could barely breathe. It was as if she'd been flash-frozen.

And then she knew why. Looking at Todd, at his handsome and now familiar face, listening to his voice, sitting in his bed after he'd just taken her on an amazingly sensual journey, she suddenly realized what she'd been ignoring all along.

He was perfect.

Well, not perfect. The man had flaws. But he was everything she'd ever been looking for. Caring, warm, smart, into family, affectionate, challenging, determined and not the least bit intimidated by her big brain.

Perfect.

And somewhere along the way, she'd fallen in love with him.

Ten

A night of incredible lovemaking managed to distract Marina from her unexpected realization. The next morning she ducked out early, claiming a very legitimate meeting with Willow. She was terrified that she wouldn't be able to keep acting normally around Todd. How could she when her brain was practically rotating from shock?

In love with Todd? How? When? She wasn't supposed to fall in love with anyone, and should the unexpected happen, did it have to be with a man who would never, ever, under any circumstances, trust a woman?

She made her way home where she showered and changed. As promised, David had dropped off her car in the night and left the keys in a planter by her front door. She collected them on her way out and drove to the bridal salon where she and Willow would pick out a couple of bridesmaid dresses to e-mail Julie.

"Nothing yucky," Willow said after Marina pulled in next to her in the salon parking lot and climbed out of her car. "Nothing too frilly, and nothing you have to be tall to look good in. I don't know if you've noticed, but I'm not tall."

Marina pretended surprise. "Since when?"

"Very funny. You know what I mean. So many clothes look fabulous if you're as tall as a giraffe but the rest of us mortals end up looking dumpy. I refuse to be dumpy at my sister's wedding."

Marina grinned. "No dumpy dresses, I promise."

"You'd better. I don't want to be outvoted by the two tall sisters."

"Trust is an important part of our relationship."

Willow narrowed her gaze. "I don't trust anyone with legs as long as yours." They walked into the salon. "I saw the wedding gown pictures. It looks great."

"I'm sure Christie will bring out the dress Julie picked," Marina said. "It's strapless, so I was thinking we could go that way, or do spaghetti straps. Nothing long."

Willow rolled her eyes. "Thank goodness. I have so many long dresses from other weddings. And the bride always said 'you can take it up.' Right. Because there are so many places I can wear a lime-green flocked short dress. Speaking of green, I know that's one of the colors, but come on. We're blond. We're doing shades of rose, aren't we?"

"Oh, yeah. Green reminds me too much of recent attack of food poisoning. I'm not wearing it."

"See. This is how it should be," Willow told her. "Sisterly solidarity."

Christie walked toward them. "Morning ladies. You must be Willow. I'm Christie."

They shook hands.

"Ready to try on bridesmaid dresses?" Christie asked. "I've been e-mailing Julie and she has a few suggestions."

Marina looked at Willow who groaned.

"Good suggestions or bad suggestions?" Willow asked, her voice small.

Christie smiled. "Good ones. I think you'll be pleased. Oh, Willow, did you want me to bring out Julie's dress so you can see it?"

"If you don't mind, that would be great."

"I'm happy to." Christie looked at Marina. "Maybe we can do the preliminary fitting, if you have time this morning."

"I'm available."

"Excellent. Now if you two will come with me, I have the dresses Julie liked picked out."

They followed her to a room on the side that was filled with bridesmaid dress samples. Two dresses were displayed on the wall. One was strapless, fitted to the waist, then flared gently to the straight hem. There was an overlayer of some sheer fabric that was scalloped at the hem. The second dress was a slip style, with a little bit of lace at the bodice and tulip hem.

Willow fingered the material on the second dress and smiled. "I think both of these work. What do you think?"

Marina nodded. "Neither are scary. I give Julie points for that."

"Good." Christie pointed to a set of dressing rooms on the far wall. "There's one for each of you inside. Why don't you try them on. I'll be back in a few minutes."

"Which means Julie e-mailed our sizes," Willow murmured when they'd slipped into the dressing rooms. "Does her level of organization ever worry you?"

"Not too much." Marina pulled off her T-shirt and unfastened her jeans. "They have shoes here that we can try on. Just to see how the dresses look in heels."

The door to her dressing room opened. Willow stepped inside and closed the door behind her.

"Okay," she said flatly. "What's wrong?"

Marina stared at her. "Nothing. Why? I'm fine."

"You're not fine. You're…" She frowned. "I don't know. I can't put my finger on it, but fine isn't applying. Are you upset? Did something bad happen? Do you need Kane to kill someone?"

"While I appreciate the offer, and I'm sure he does, too, I'm good. Really."

Willow folded her arms over her chest. "I'm not leaving until you confess everything."

"There's nothing to…" Marina sighed. "I'd been so determined to act normal, too."

"You didn't quite make the goal." Willow's mouth twisted. "What happened? Is it Todd? Did he hurt you?"

"No. Of course not. He didn't do anything wrong. It's just…"

Willow moved closer and touched her arm. "You don't have to talk about it if you don't want to."

Marina managed a smile. "Oh, sure. Say that now. I just… We…" She swallowed. "I'm in love with him."

Willow continued to stare at her. "And?"

"And nothing. Isn't that enough? I'm in love with Todd Aston the Third. How crazy is that?"

Willow grinned, then hugged her. "Not crazy at all. It's great. You're in love. You're single, he's single. You're amazing, he might be someone the rest of the family can tolerate. What's the problem?"

Marina sank onto the bench in the room and covered her face with her hands. "I'm terrified. What if I'm just like Mom? What if I get lost? What if I let him treat me horribly and I pretend it's enough because it's better than being without him?"

Willow sank down next to her. "What if you don't?" she asked as she put her arm around Marina. "What if you're strong and grown-up and you just let yourself be happy?"

While she appreciated the support, happy didn't seem like much of an option. "He has issues."

Willow rolled her eyes. "Of course he does. All men do."

"His are complicated. He doesn't trust women. At all. Ever. No female trusting by the rich guy."

"Sounds simple to me," Willow said. "Fine. He doesn't trust. I'm sure other women have taught him that. But what have you ever done to make him not trust you? Nothing. So it may take some time and a little work, but you'll bring him around."

Marina wished it was that easy, but something in her gut told her that Todd wasn't going to be convinced by a lack of action on her part.

"Have you always been this optimistic?" she asked.

"I think so," Willow told her. "I'm the middle child. It's my job to see both sides of things. Although in this case, I'm only seeing yours. Have a little faith. I doubt your feelings are one-sided. You're pretty amazing. He's lucky to have you in his life."

"I don't think I'm the problem. He is and I don't know how to fix that."

"You don't have to. That's his job."

Marina looked at her sister. "I'm not like Mom, am I? Falling for a guy who can't commit?"

"You're nothing like Mom. You are your own person. Have a little faith in yourself."

Faith sounded easy enough, but Marina wasn't sure how to put it into play.

"You okay?" Willow asked.

Marina nodded. "We have dresses to try on."

A few minutes later they met by the large three-way mirror.

"This is not flattering," Willow grumbled as she tugged on the spaghetti straps of her dress. "The tulip hem thingy makes me look short."

"You are short," Marina teased. "But the dress isn't the right one. We both looked better in the strapless one. I hope Julie doesn't mind that the waist is so fitted."

Willow grinned. "You mean she'll be bitter because her tummy is growing? Hmmm. I hadn't thought of that. But it's okay. She can be bitter for a while. She's getting a baby." She smoothed the front of her dress. "After Kane and I get married, we're going to try for children right away. I'm really excited. I feel like I had my first taste of pregnancy the first couple of weeks I was on the pill."

"Bloated?" Marina asked sympathetically. "That's why I'm not on it. Plus, I felt yucky."

"Me, too. But the yucky part passed. Good things, too, because of the whole condom problem."

Marina stared at her. "What condom problem?"

"You know. That they're not a hundred percent. If used perfectly, in controlled studies, they're like ninety-seven percent effective. But in real world use, it's a lot lower than that."

Willow kept on talking, but Marina wasn't listening.

Less effective? As in more chance of getting pregnant?

All she and Todd had used were condoms. She wasn't on anything else and he'd never asked. Not that there was a whole lot more he could have done, but still.

She touched her stomach and tried to relax. So they weren't a hundred percent. She and Todd had only made love a few times. Nothing could have happened. Not really. Could it?

Two and a half long hours later, Marina finally escaped the bridal shop. She'd had to suffer through the wedding gown fitting, which Willow had stayed for. In the end she, Marina, had gotten away only to drive to a drugstore and buy two different pregnancy tests. She was positive she was fine, but a little scientific evidence never hurt.

Now she counted out days on her calendar and had to admit that maybe she was a little late. Just by a couple of days, but still.

Her chest tightened until she found it hard to breathe. Pregnant? She couldn't be. Not that she didn't want kids, but not now. Not like this.

She remembered all the horror stories Todd had shared. If she were pregnant, he would think she was just like the other women in his life. He would never trust her.

Scared, shaking and terrified of the outcome, she opened both boxes and took the test. When the needed time has passed, she stared down at two plastic sticks and groaned.

One said she was pregnant, the other one didn't.

"Just so how my day is going," she said, fighting tears of frustration. "I have to know."

She grabbed the first of the boxes and dialed the 800 number for customer service.

"Hi," she said, when a woman answered. "I took one of your pregnancy tests a few minutes ago. I also took another brand. Your test says I'm not pregnant and theirs says I am. Who should I believe?"

"Oh, no," the other woman said. "That's not good. How late are you?"

"Just a couple of days."

"Okay, you have a couple of choices. You can buy more tests and see what they say, or you can wait. I know it's hard, but that would be my advice. Wait about a week and take the tests again. Your final option is to make an appointment with your doctor."

Marina thanked the woman and hung up. Going to her doctor wasn't an option. He was practically a friend of the family and her mother worked in his office. That was a little too close to home for this situation. She could find another doctor, but by the time they fit her in, at least a week would have passed anyway. Waiting and taking the tests again made the most sense.

But being sensible didn't ease the knot in her stomach to make her breathe any easier. Pregnant? Was it possible?

She was torn between the maternal thrill of a baby and the horror of knowing what Todd would think about her. That she'd tricked him.

Needing to talk to someone, she picked up the phone and called Willow.

Her sister's cell went right to voice mail, which meant Willow was probably with Kane and they were practicing for making babies of their own.

Restless and still needing to talk, Marina walked to her laptop and turned it on.

To: Julie_Nelson@SGC.usa
From: Marina_Nelson@mynetwork.LA.com
Hi. It's the middle of the day here, so I'm thinking it's the middle of the night there. Which is a serious drag because I really need to talk. Not that we will, and I don't want you to call. It's about a billion dollars

a minute and I'll be in class most of tomorrow. It's just...

Okay—don't be drinking your morning coffee when you read this. I'm late. As in...late. So I got a couple of pregnancy tests and took them. One says I'm pregnant, one says I'm not. The lady at the company suggested I wait another week and retest, which really makes sense. Except wait a week to know? How is that possible?

I want kids. I really wouldn't mind being pregnant—except for Todd. He's not a trusting guy and while I don't blame him, I can't begin to imagine what he would say if I told him I was pregnant. He would think I was trying to manipulate him or trick him. It would be awful.

Even worse...and you can't tell anyone about any of this, but especially what I'm about to say. I think I'm in love with him.

Marina paused in her typing, then sighed.

No. That's wrong. I know I'm in love with him. I've been in love with him for a while now. Maybe from the beginning. I'm excited and scared. I mean, what if I'm like Mom? But what if I'm not? What if I can't be strong? So that's a good possibility. But this is Todd. Would he ever trust me enough to have a real relationship? Is he even interested in a real relationship? And if he could be, being pregnant will ruin everything.

So that's how my day is going. E-mail me back

when you can. I feel better now that we've "talked." Thanks for listening.

* * *

Marina didn't sleep much that night, which made her morning class on the physical aspects of Inorganic Chemistry class tough. She did her best to clear her mind of all that was currently going on in her life and pay attention to the lecture. She seemed to do okay, because Jason, one of her deaf students, only frowned at her twice.

When class ended, she made arrangements to meet him in the lab later that week, then walked toward her car. As she moved through the crowd of students, her mind swirled and dipped and raced in a hundred different directions.

What if she was pregnant? How would she tell Todd? What if she wasn't? Would she be sad?

She felt her emotions being ripped in two. She loved Todd and would be thrilled to be having a baby with him. But with his past, she doubted they could ever get past his inherent mistrust of all women, including her. So the most sensible thing to hope was that there was no baby. Except she couldn't quite bring herself to want that.

Sleep, she thought as she walked across the parking lot. She needed sleep.

What she got was a familiar expensive convertible pulling up next to her. The driver's window rolled down and a very angry-looking Todd stared at her.

"Get in," he said flatly. "We have to talk."

Eleven

He knew. She could read it in the coldness in his eyes.

Marina wasn't surprised. There was no way Julie wouldn't have told Ryan, and Ryan and Todd were as close as brothers.

"I'll follow you to your place," she said, knowing there was a very good chance that any conversation with Todd right now wasn't going to go well. Better to be able to leave and not have to wait for him to drive her anywhere.

He opened his mouth, but before she could speak, she added, "I'll follow you there. You should at least trust me that much."

"Why?" he asked bluntly. But he also closed the window and drove a few feet forward so she could back out her car.

Twenty minutes later she drove onto the familiar circular stone driveway in front of the massive house she'd actually grown to like. But as she climbed out her car, she felt an uncomfortable combination of apprehension and panic. Based on all that she knew about him, Todd wasn't going to handle any of this well.

They walked inside without saying anything. She figured that she should probably be the one to start the conversation, but she didn't know how. Nor did she know what he knew. Which might be a good place to start.

She followed Todd into his study and set her purse on one of the leather chairs in the book-lined space.

"Did Ryan give you a recap or just forward my mail?" she asked, suddenly remembering her confession of love. Surely Julie hadn't shared that with her fiancé.

"He gave me the facts." Todd's dark gaze dropped to her midsection. "That you think you're pregnant."

She couldn't figure out what he was thinking from his tone. So far, his body language seemed controlled enough, so she should be feeling better. Except she wasn't. There was a coldness, a bitterness, that seemed to steal all the warmth from the room. Despite the pleasant temperature, she found herself shivering.

"I don't know if I am," she said. "He told you about the two pregnancy tests?"

Todd moved behind his desk, then turned to face her. "Let me be clear. I've been manipulated by women far more experienced than you, Marina. You will not win this game."

She felt as if she'd been slapped. "I'm not playing a

game. How could I be? I'm not like that and you know it. You know *me*, Todd."

"Do I? You're the one who's in this for a million dollars."

She stared at him. "Don't be ridiculous. That's just a crazy idea of Ruth's."

"She offered to take the money off the table, but you told her no."

Coldness eased down her spine. "I was kidding. It was a joke."

Nothing in his expression hinted that he believed her. The walls seemed to close in a little.

She took a step toward him. "This is crazy. We've become friends. We've laughed together, we'd talked about our hopes and dreams. I'm not some manipulating bitch out for the money. Dammit, Todd, I didn't trap you. You wanted us to make love, too. You were a more than willing participant."

He opened a desk drawer and pulled out a pad of paper. "If you continue to claim to be pregnant, I'll want the condition confirmed by an independent test performed by a doctor of my choosing. I will be there for the test, as will my attorney."

"Claim to be pregnant?" she asked, her voice low and shaky. "I'm saying I don't know. How much more honest can I be?"

He ignored that, too.

"If you are pregnant, I want paternity determined by a DNA test upon birth. If I am the father, we'll have to negotiate some kind of custody arrangement." He stared at her. "I wouldn't count on winning that battle if I were you."

It was like being locked in a freezer. The chill made it nearly impossible to breathe.

She closed her eyes as she remembered his words about wanting children, but not a mother. Was that really his plan? To take her baby?

"This isn't about me," she told him. "None of this is. This is about your past. You're making me pay for what those other women did to you."

"Did my aunt offer to withdraw the million dollars?" he asked.

She couldn't win. He wouldn't let her. "Yes."

"Did you tell her to keep it on the table."

"Yes."

There was no point in explaining she'd been kidding. That she'd never imagined even liking him, let alone falling for him.

"It's like asking for the moon," she said, even as she knew she was wasting breath and energy. "Sure, I said I'd take it but it was like accepting an offer to raise the Titanic. It's not going to happen. The money isn't real."

She took another step toward him, although with a giant desk between them, it was a pretty useless gesture.

"I wanted to give my sister a great wedding," she said. "Just like you wanted to give that to Ryan. We had to work together. At first I didn't like you very much, but then we became friends and it was great. That's all, Todd. Don't make it ugly now."

"Give me one reason why I should trust you."

"You can't argue trust. It has to be earned over time. Tell me one thing I've done to violate your trust."

"I can give you a million of them. You getting pregnant only confirms what you wanted all along."

Horror swept through her. "It was a joke," she began, then stopped. What was the point?

She grabbed her purse and pulled out her cell phone. Ruth's number was in her address book. She hit Send.

"Hi, it's Marina," she said, when Ruth had answered. "I need to tell you I'm not interested in the million dollars. Whatever happens, I don't want it."

Her grandmother sighed. "You never did want it, dear. I knew that."

"Todd doesn't."

"Oh, yes. He can be stubborn. But he'll come around."

Marina stared at his stern expression, at the starkness in his eyes. "I'm not so sure about that."

"I know he seems like he's too much work, but he'll be worth it in the end. Have a little faith."

"I'll try." She hung up.

Faith. Was there enough of that in the world?

"It doesn't mean anything," he told her. "You know you can get even more money from me."

And then she got it. She couldn't win. That was the point.

"If it wasn't the pregnancy concern, it would have been something else," she said, more to herself than him. "You're determined to never trust me and people always find what they go looking for. If you expect the worst, you'll find it."

She drew in a breath. "Someday I'll appreciate the irony of this situation. I've been so worried about being like my mother. I've been terrified I'll lose myself in a man. I never stopped to think about the danger of falling for someone who couldn't love me back. In my head, I was the one with the big problem."

She shoved her cell phone into her jeans pocket and grabbed her purse. "But I'm not. I was willing to risk it with you. I was scared and worried, but still willing to take on that next step. I never stopped to think all my fears didn't matter. Because you're not willing."

His expression didn't change. She wasn't sure why she was explaining herself, except maybe for some kind of closure.

"The only way to convince you I'm not in it for the money is to not be pregnant and never see you again," she said. "I can't do anything about having or not having a baby, but I can get out of your life. If I really am pregnant, we'll work something out. Something fair. You're not going to simply take my child. If I'm not, then we only have to deal with each other at the wedding and then stay out of each other's lives."

She walked to the study door, then turned back. "I know you're scared, Todd. I'm scared, too. But after falling in love with you, I'm willing to face my fears. Maybe I'm not the one for you. Maybe you don't want to care about me, and that's fine. But if you never care about anyone, the bitches of the world win. They might not have you, but they've sure made sure no one else will, either. It's a hell of a way for you to live."

* * *

He waited until he heard the front door close before walking out of the study. The emptiness of the house pressed down on him, but was nothing when compared to the fury he felt at her betrayal. If there was one woman he was going to trust, it would have been Marina. Only she'd turned out to be just like the rest of them.

Pregnant, he thought grimly. Fine. If she wanted to play that game, he would play it right back. He would take the baby and start the family he'd always wanted. She would be compensated, but nothing else.

She was, he acknowledged, a good genetic candidate for his child's mother. Intelligent, healthy, determined. He would hire a nanny and be a father.

It was a plan and he always felt better when he had a plan. But not today. He had a hole in his chest and it burned.

He wanted to throw something. He wanted to put his fist through a wall. He wanted her not to be like them. He wanted to trust her.

Which he couldn't.

He might have given her a second chance if she'd confessed and then begged for his understanding. If she hadn't said she loved him. Because that was the biggest betrayal of all. To use the one thing he truly wanted to manipulate him. That he could never forgive.

Marina knew she would probably drown in her tears. They came and came, pouring down her face as sobs ripped through her body. The pain was more intense than anything she'd ever experienced. It was as if she'd been cut off from the very air she needed to survive. Only she didn't die. She just hurt and cried and prayed to feel better.

Willow held her and soothed her with soft sounds. Not words. There were no words.

"How do I stop loving him?" Marina asked, her throat raw, her body battered. "Tell me how."

"I don't know," Willow admitted softly. "But we'll figure out a way."

Nearly a week later, Todd walked into the florist to finalize the order for the flowers. While he wanted to make sure the wedding looked good for Ryan and Julie, most of his attention was on the fact that he was going to see Marina again.

He'd expected her to call and she hadn't. So what did that mean? She'd claimed to love him and then she'd disappeared. If she loved him, shouldn't she be trying to get him back?

He wanted her to be trying and it really pissed him off that she hadn't once been in touch with him. As he'd been the point of contact with the florist, he'd been forced to call Marina to set up their appointment. Even more annoying, he'd been disappointed when he'd gotten her machine.

He'd done the right thing—leaving a message rather than trying again later. But she hadn't phoned him back and now, as he stood surrounded by flowers, he found himself looking forward to seeing her again.

He knew he shouldn't. He knew she was screwing with him, but that didn't stop the anticipation from rising inside of him.

She walked in, right on time for their appointment.

Even as he held himself still and didn't say anything, his body reacted to her nearness. She was beautiful, in a stern, pale kind of way. His fingers itched to get lost in her long gold-blond hair. He ached to touched her all over, to listen to her voice, to hear her laugh. He wanted to lean in and inhale the scent of her body.

Damn. What was wrong with him? He knew better. Look at what she'd done.

Except what had she done? Thought she might be pregnant? As she'd pointed out, he'd been more than willing to sleep with her. They'd used protection, but it didn't always work. Weren't they equally to blame for what happened? Did he really believe that Marina was trying to trick him?

"I have a class in an hour," she told him. "So why don't you go head and make the final selection on the flowers?" She handed him a few printed out e-mails. "These are Julie's ideas for her bouquets. I'm sure Beatrice can come up with something beautiful."

"You're not staying?" he asked, knowing he sounded like an idiot. Oddly he'd counted on them spending the afternoon together.

"No. I can't miss class. I know the wedding is next week, but everything else is taken care of. Julie and Ryan will be back this weekend."

She glanced around, as if checking to make sure they were alone, then she lowered her voice. "The mixed message has been resolved. I'm not pregnant."

"You took the tests again?"

"I didn't have to."

There wasn't a baby. Nothing about her expression told him what she was thinking, but he was shocked to feel the ache of sadness sweep through him.

Sad? Why should he be sad? Because he'd secretly wanted a baby with Marina?

"I'm sure you're relieved," she told him. "I know I am. Not that I wouldn't have loved to have a baby. Just not with you."

Her words did what they were supposed to. They cut through him, wounding.

"Under the circumstances," he began.

She shook her head. "I'll accept you being upset. Anyone would be. I'll even accept that you have issues, but there is no excuse for what you said and how you treated me. You threatened to take my child. You accused me of lying deliberately for financial gain. You made judgments and decisions before you knew all the facts. You were wrong about me, Todd. So very wrong. I was never in it for the money."

She squared her shoulders. "The thing that hurts the most is that I think you knew you were wrong, too. I think you secretly did believe me, but you couldn't admit it. So you attacked. That's not something I can get over. I suppose the only bright spot in all of this is that I was wrong about you, too. I was wrong to think you were special. I was wrong to think you were the kind of man I could fall in love with."

And as she had before, she walked out and left him alone.

But this time was different. This time as she left, he realized the enormity of what he'd lost. That despite the pregnancy, his past, her worries and all that had happened between them, that he'd fallen in love with her.

But he realized it too late. As he'd once told her— what had happened was unforgivable.

Twelve

Tuesday after work, Todd sorted through the mail. There was a large, stiff envelope with no return address on the bottom of the pile.

He opened it and removed several photographs. The pictures they'd taken at Belinda's studio. Samples, to send to Julie and Ryan. Apparently Belinda had decided to send him copies.

He pulled out the eight-by-ten pictures and studied them. Marina stood in his arms, staring up at him, her mouth curved in a smile. He stared down at her with an intensity that made him wonder what he'd been thinking.

There was an ease in their pose, and a connection. The camera had captured what he'd never allowed himself to see before—how he and Marina seemed to belong together.

There was something else in the pictures. Something in her blue eyes. Love.

He flipped through the six photographs, then carried them into his study and sat behind his desk. After turning on the lamp, he laid out pictures and let the images speak for themselves.

There was a hint of laughter in one, sexual need in another. A smile that spoke of a shared secret.

The pain slammed into him with the subtly of a lightning bolt. It cut through him, leaving him exposed and bleeding. Something dark and ugly surrounded his soul and began to squeeze the life out of him.

He'd lost her. He'd been so sure he would never want anyone that he'd made the decision to let her go before he'd even known what it was to have her. He'd assumed she wouldn't matter, couldn't be special. He'd cast off her gift of love without being aware that it could change him forever.

Now, alone, he felt the loss of her. He ached to hear her laughter, to see her smile, to touch her, hold her. He wanted her to need him—not just in bed, but in her life. He wanted her to miss him, to grow old with him. To love him.

He returned the pictures to the envelope. She'd made it pretty damn clear that she wasn't interested in him anymore. That she didn't love him.

He closed his eyes for a second, then opened them. Marina wasn't someone to give her heart lightly. Was it possible that she'd just been able to turn off her feelings or had she been bluffing because anything else hurt too much. Was there still a chance?

He pushed to his feet and realized it didn't matter about chances or hopes or wishes. He'd always been a man who worked his ass off to get what he wanted. If he'd been willing to give that much to something as meaningless as a business, what more would he be willing to do to convince the only woman he'd ever loved to take a chance on him?

Marina was making coffee when she heard a knock on her front door. She instantly thought it was Todd, crawling back to beg her to give him another chance. The visual would have been funny, if her reaction hadn't been so incredibly sad. Even knowing what he was and how badly he'd handled the situation, she desperately wanted to give him another chance. Which made her a huge weenie.

But it didn't stop her heart from fluttering in anticipation as she pulled open the door. And while the person standing there wasn't Todd, it was nearly as good.

"Julie! You're back!"

Marina reached for her sister just as Julie grabbed for her. They hugged and screamed and danced in front of the open door, then Marina stepped back to study the changes of the past six weeks.

"You're barely showing," she said, staring at her sister's nonexistent bump. "But you look so happy."

It was true. Julie's face glowed with contentment.

"I am happy," her sister told her. "Ryan and I got back last night and I wanted to come see you first thing. How are you?"

Marina led the way into the apartment. "I'm good. Fine."

Julie didn't look convinced. "You can't be fine."

"Okay—how about I'm adjusting? Would that work?"

"Maybe." Julie hugged her again. "Are you sorry about the baby?"

"Yes and no. I was excited at the thought of being pregnant. Terrified, but excited. Then when Todd freaked, I knew having a child with him would be a big mistake. He's not ready to trust anyone. I can't have a relationship with a guy who's so willing to think the worst of me. I certainly can't have a baby with him. So not being pregnant is a good thing, right?"

Marina did her best to speak calmly, to be logical and rational and sensible about the whole thing. But in truth, her heart hurt. She missed Todd, she missed the baby, which was insane and she didn't know when she was going to be able to get back to her old self.

"Oh, Marina," Julie murmured. "I'm so sorry. About all of it. I shouldn't have asked you two to work on the wedding."

Marina took her hand and led her to the sofa. They plopped down at opposite corners.

"You had nothing to do with this," Marina told her honestly. "Todd and I are totally responsible for what happened. I thought I was safe from anyone like him. He's so not my type."

"Apparently he is," Julie told her.

"Tell me about it. The thing is, we were attracted, we acted on that attraction and I screwed up. I thought it was more than it was. It ended badly, but at least I know the truth about him. I won't spend my time missing a man who can never be what I need."

"So you're over him?" Julie asked, sounding doubtful.

"I'm working on it. The good news is if I fell in love with him, I can fall in love with someone else. It will just take a little time."

"As easy as that?"

"I don't think it will be easy." She thought about Todd, about how he made her laugh and how they were more alike than she ever would have guessed. "I miss him. I'll miss him for a long time, but I'll recover, and then I'll move on."

To what? Another man? She couldn't imagine ever caring about anyone the way she cared about Todd. Worse, even though she would never admit it to another living creature, she finally understood her mother. In truth, she, Marina, would also settle for a small piece of Todd rather than having no part of him at all. Thank goodness no one was giving her the option.

"What about the wedding and the rehearsal and the rehearsal dinner?" Julie asked. "Will that be too awful for you? Would you rather not come?"

Marina shook her head. "It's your wedding. Of course I'll be there. I love you and I want to see you and Ryan get married. Plus, hey, I have a whole lot invested in the event."

"But Todd…"

"I can handle it," she promised, hoping it was true. "It's one evening and one day. I'm tough. Don't worry about me. Just focus on yourself and your happy day. You're marrying Ryan."

Julie smiled with so much love, she lit up the room. "I know. I can't believe I was so lucky to find him. Thank you for all you've done. Thank you for making my wedding perfect."

Marina had to blink several times to fight tears. "Don't thank me yet. You haven't seen anything. You did say you wanted a jungle theme for the reception, right? Because we found the cutest little stuffed giraffes for wedding favors, not to mention a 'sounds of the jungle' CD to play at the reception."

Julie swallowed hard. "You didn't. You wouldn't."

"You'll have to wait and see."

The rehearsal dinner was held on the Thursday before the wedding. Marina spent most of the afternoon in hot curlers in a feeble attempt to get her long hair to be something other than straight.

She usually didn't bother, but today she felt compelled. Probably because she was going to have to spend several hours in Todd's company and she was bitter enough to want to look good enough to make him feel bad. Not exactly her proudest moment.

She was also scared about seeing him. At the florist, she'd been able to keep the meeting short and maintain control. While the wedding rehearsal itself didn't worry her, the dinner was another matter. It was just going to be family—Julie, Ryan, Willow, Kane, Todd and herself, their mom, Ruth plus Todd and Ryan's parents.

That meant a small table and lots of conversation. Everyone would notice if she was too quiet or if she and Todd weren't speaking. It could be awkward and embarrassing. Plus her mother didn't know anything about her relationship with Todd…unless Ruth had shared that information with her, as well as Julie.

Marina groaned at the thought, then slipped on her dress and zipped it up the back.

The dark blue fabric brought out the color of her eyes and the fitted style made her feel especially skinny. She'd already finished her makeup so all that was left was her hair.

She took out all the curlers, then bent over at the waist and began to finger-comb the curls. When they were loose and, hopefully, sexy-looking, she stretched out her arm to grab for the hairspray, but instead encountered a hand.

She immediately screamed, jerked into an upright position and took a jump back.

Todd stood next to her dresser in her bedroom. Her messy bedroom with the unmade bed and clothes scattered everywhere. Although when compared with how fast and hard her heart pounded in her chest, she wasn't sure that mattered.

She had a brief impression of how great he looked in khakis and a silk shirt, then remembered her hair and clamped both hands on top of her head.

"What are you doing here?" she asked. "How did you get in? Couldn't you have knocked?"

At least she was dressed, but jeez. Talk about a shock.

"I knocked several times, then tried the door. It was open. You okay?"

No, she wasn't. She risked a glance in the mirror and saw her hair didn't look too bad, so she lowered her hands to her sides.

"You shouldn't leave your door unlocked," he said.

"You drove all the way out here to tell me that? Fine. I shouldn't. I don't normally. I don't know why I did today."

Distraction, she thought. She'd been distracted at the thought of seeing him, and now that he was standing in front of her, she knew why.

She still loved him. Despite everything he'd said and all that had happened and how much she should know better, she loved him. Right this second, she wanted to throw herself into his arms and have him tell her that they would work it out. That what had happened before had been nothing more than an icky misunderstanding. Not that Todd would ever say "icky."

"Why are you here?" she asked.

"I wanted to talk to you," he told her. "There are some things we have to clear up."

Right. The rehearsal dinner. "I'm fine with it," she said, hoping she would be. "Yes, it will be awkward with our family there. I've been thinking about everything and I think we can pull this off. It's not like we were dating for years. No one really knows. Well, my sisters and Ruth, but they won't say anything. We planned the wedding together, nothing more."

His dark gaze settled on her face. "Is that all that happened?"

"It's all I'm going to admit to."

"I'm giving a toast tonight. At the dinner. I would appreciate it if you'd listen to it and tell me where I can improve it."

He wanted her advice? Even worse, she was pathetic enough to be willing to give it.

"Fine. Read away."

He pulled a piece of paper out of his shirt pocket and unfolded it. "The Bible tells us that love is kind. Scholars tell us that love can change the course of history. Scientists tell us that love is chemical. Poets tell us that love is eternal. But true love is so much more than that. It's about believing and risking. It's about committing to always being there for one person and believing that person will be there for you. Love is about hanging on through the roller-coaster ride of life. Love is having faith, in yourself and the person you love. For Julie and Ryan, love is who they are."

His words wrapped around her like a hug. She wanted to both laugh and cry, but mostly she wanted to go to him and tell him that no matter what, she would always love him. That's what love was for her. How had he known?

Instead she said, "It's lovely. They'll be deeply touched."

He took a step toward her. "I mean it. For a long time I didn't know what to say about them getting married.

I thought Ryan was a fool for trusting Julie. Eventually she won me over and I was happy for him. But not envious. I never wanted what he had…until now." He smiled wryly. "Not Julie—the in-love part."

"Good to know," she managed to say even though her throat felt tight. What was he saying? That he cared? That he wanted to care? That she mattered?

"You know my past," he said. "You know why I hold myself back, never really getting emotionally involved. You know what I'm afraid of." He shook his head. "I can't believe I just admitted I'm afraid."

Neither could she. "I do know why."

"When you said you were pregnant, I thought you were just like them," he said, staring into her eyes. "I was angry, but more at me than at you. I was angry at myself for wanting you to be different. For wanting to believe you hadn't tricked me. I said a lot of things I shouldn't have said. I was wrong. Because you're not like them."

Her eyes filled with tears, but she blinked them away. He took a step toward her.

"Marina, when you told me there wasn't a baby, I was devastated. I want to have children with you. I love you. I want to marry you and grow old with you. I want to live with you in that damn house of mine and have you change everything in my world. I want to believe in forever."

She was already on the emotional edge, barely able to believe he was actually speaking these words to her.

Then he stunned her by dropping to one knee, taking her hand in his and asking, "Can you forgive me? Can you give me another chance? Will you take that step of faith and believe in me? Will you marry me?"

She didn't mean to burst into tears, but she did. She also managed to nod and that must have been enough because then Todd was standing and pulling her close. She went into his embrace and knew she would always feel safe when she was with him.

He held her tightly against him. "I love you," he whispered into her ear. "I think I've loved you from the first. It was safe to be friends and so I let down my guard. One day I woke up and you were a part of me. I'm so sorry for what I said, how I reacted."

"It's okay. I understand." She looked at him and smiled through her tears. "I love you, too."

He wiped her face with his fingers. "I'm glad you didn't change your mind."

"I wanted to, but I couldn't. I seem to be a one-man woman."

"Thank God."

She laughed and so did he. Then he kissed her. At the first brush of his mouth, her whole world righted itself.

"We need to get to the rehearsal," he said when they came up for air. "But first..."

He pulled a small box out of his slacks front pocket. "This belonged to my grandmother. If you don't like it, we can pick out something else."

He opened the box and she gasped. Nestled in the velvet lining was a sparkling diamond ring. A huge, round center stone was surrounded by other diamonds. The light glinted off the facets and nearly blinded her.

"It's beautiful," she whispered, "but it's really…"

"Big?" He grinned. "We Astons don't do anything by halves. It's about eight carats total."

"Wow."

"Too much?"

"I'll adjust."

He slipped the ring on her finger and it fit perfectly.

"It was meant for you," he said just before he kissed her. "I love you, Marina."

"I love you, too." She gave herself up to his embrace, then pulled back. "Does this mean there's going to be a Todd Aston the Fourth?"

"Probably."

"I can live with that." She glanced down at her ring, then pulled it off her finger.

He nodded. "After the wedding?"

"If that's okay. I don't want to take away the spotlight from Julie and Ryan."

"I'm good with that. We have our whole lives to celebrate."

He set the box on her dresser and she put the ring into the box. Then they walked out together.

"I have some very specific ideas about our wedding," he said as she collected her purse. "Color schemes. Place settings."

She laughed. "So you think we should plan it together?"

"We did a good job on this one. We're a great team."

"Yes, we are."

* * * * *

Don't miss HER LAST FIRST DATE,
the third book in the Special Edition miniseries
POSITIVELY PREGNANT
By bestselling author Susan Mallery
On sale June 2007
wherever Silhouette Books are sold.

Happily ever after is just the beginning...

Turn the page for a sneak preview of
DANCING ON SUNDAY AFTERNOONS
by
Linda Cardillo

*Harlequin Everlasting—Every great love
has a story to tell.* ™
*A brand-new line from Harlequin Books
launching this February!*

Prologue

Giulia D'Orazio
1983

I had two husbands—Paolo and Salvatore.

Salvatore and I were married for thirty-two years. I still live in the house he bought for us; I still sleep in our bed. All around me are the signs of our life together. My bedroom window looks out over the garden he planted. In the middle of the city, he coaxed tomatoes, peppers, zucchini—even grapes for his wine—out of the ground. On weekends, he used to drive up to his cousin's farm in Waterbury and bring back manure. In the winter, he wrapped the peach tree and the fig tree with rags and black rubber hoses against the cold, his massive, coarse hands gentling those trees as if they were his fragile-skinned babies. My neighbor, Dominic Grazza, does that for me now. My boys have no time for the garden.

In the front of the house, Salvatore planted roses. The roses I take care of myself. They are giant, cream-colored, fragrant. In the afternoons, I like to sit out on the porch with my coffee, protected from the eyes of the neighborhood by that curtain of flowers.

Salvatore died in this house thirty-five years ago. In the last months, he lay on the sofa in the parlor so he could be in the middle of everything. Except for the two oldest boys, all the children were still at home and we ate together every evening. Salvatore could see the dining room table from the sofa, and he could hear everything that was said. "I'm not dead, yet," he told me. "I want to know what's going on."

When my first grandchild, Cara, was born, we brought her to him, and he held her on his chest, stroking her tiny head. Sometimes they fell asleep together.

Over on the radiator cover in the corner of the parlor is the portrait Salvatore and I had taken on our twenty-fifth anniversary. This brooch I'm wearing today, with the diamonds—I'm wearing it in the photograph also—Salvatore gave it to me that day. Upstairs on my dresser is a jewelry box filled with necklaces and bracelets and earrings. All from Salvatore.

I am surrounded by the things Salvatore gave me, or did for me. But, God forgive me, as I lie alone now in my bed, it is Paolo I remember.

Paolo left me nothing. Nothing, that is, that my family, especially my sisters, thought had any value. No house. No diamonds. Not even a photograph.

But after he was gone, and I could catch my breath from the pain, I knew that I still had something. In the middle of the night, I sat alone and held them in my hands, reading the words over and over until I heard his voice in my head. I had Paolo's letters.

* * * * *

Be sure to look for
DANCING ON SUNDAY AFTERNOONS
available January 30, 2007.
And look, too, for our other
Everlasting title available, FALL FROM GRACE
by Kristi Gold.

FALL FROM GRACE is a deeply emotional story
of what a long-term love really means.
As Jack and Anne Morgan discover,
marriage vows can be broken—
but they can be mended, too.
And the memories of their marriage
have an unexpected power to bring back a love
that never really left....

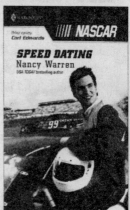

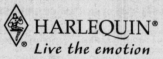

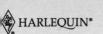

HARLEQUIN®

EVERLASTING LOVE™

Every great love has a story to tell™

Save $1.⁰⁰ off

the purchase of any Harlequin Everlasting Love novel

Coupon valid from January 1, 2007 until April 30, 2007.

Valid at retail outlets in the U.S. only. Limit one coupon per customer.

5 65373 00076 2   (8100) 0 11302

HEUSCPN0407

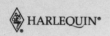

HARLEQUIN®

E V E R L A S T I N G   L O V E ™

Every great love has a story to tell ™

Save $1.⁰⁰ off

the purchase of
any Harlequin
Everlasting Love novel

Coupon valid from January 1, 2007
until April 30, 2007.

Valid at retail outlets in Canada only.
Limit one coupon per customer.

52607370

HECDNCPN0407

What a month!

In February watch for

Rancher and Protector
Part of the Western Weddings miniseries
BY JUDY CHRISTENBERRY

The Boss's Pregnancy Proposal
BY RAYE MORGAN

Also in February, expect
MORE of what you love
as the Harlequin Romance line
increases to six titles per month.